# Emma's Hands

# Emma's Hands

## by Mary Swan

The Porcupine's Quill

National Library of Canada Cataloguing in Publication Data

Swan, Mary, 1953 –
Emma's hands/Mary Swan.

Short stories.
ISBN 0-88984-268-x

I. Title.

PS8587.W344E55 2003    C813'.6    C2003-905020-3

1  2  3  4  •  05  04  03

Published by The Porcupine's Quill,
68 Main Street, Erin, Ontario NOB 1TO.
www.sentex.net/~pql

Readied for the press by John Metcalf; copy edited by Doris Cowan.
Typeset in Bauer Bodoni, printed on Zephyr Antique laid
and bound at the Porcupine's Quill.

We acknowledge the support of the Ontario Arts Council,
and the Canada Council for the Arts for our publishing program.
The financial support of the Government of Canada
through the Book Publishing Industry Development Program
is also gratefully acknowledged. Thanks, also, to the Government of
Ontario through the Ontario Media Development Corporation's
Ontario Book Initiative.

Canada Council
for the Arts

Conseil des Arts
du Canada

ONTARIO ARTS COUNCIL
CONSEIL DES ARTS DE L'ONTARIO

Canada

For Barb, Sue, Bill and Mike

# Table of Contents

# Hour of Lead

This is what she thought in the space of the spoon, in the space between the *tap-tap* on the edge of the bowl and the light touch on her lower lip. She thought, I must get out of here; she thought, I will never get out of here.

The spoon reminded her of things, and it reminded her of being reminded. How one time, washing the curved handle of an old baby spoon, she had suddenly smelled woodsmoke, had seen her mother's hand and the shadowed place where her face was, light bursting all around. This, she believed, was her earliest memory. And that reminded her of another time, feeding Raymond in his chair. How he kept grabbing at the spoon, laughing and splattering food about, and how she had finally shouted and banged it down with great force. His sudden round eyes and the crackle of the letter in her apron pocket as she scooped him up and held him close, both of them howling then. It was the letter, of course, it was Hugh, of course; it always was in those days.

She told Raymond everything in his first long months, while he kicked his fat legs in the crib or banged pots together, sitting on the kitchen floor. Crooned Hugh's name through the darkest part of the night, rocking him back to sleep. Until having told it all she found that she could fold it up and put it away, like the letters, only stumble across it now and then, as she did with them, in the time that was the rest of her life.

She wondered who would find the letters now, and what they would make of them. Perhaps nothing; you had to read between the lines, after all. You had to know the look of the hand that held the pen, the exact way the lips would move with the words; you had to know what came before, and after. Still, there were times when it had mattered a great deal that someone would know about them. The envelopes with the Bolivian stamps cut off — what had she done with those? The letters themselves in another long envelope marked *Bills*. The disintegrating rubber bands that she replaced each time she came across them.

Once she bought a new coat, fine dark green wool, and when one of her granddaughters came to visit she said, 'Try it on, see how it looks.' And the girl slipped her arms into the sleeves, shook her long hair free of the collar, and Amelia stood behind her, lifting the last strands of hair and looking over her shoulder into the mirror on the opened door. 'It suits you, that coat,' she said. 'You should have it, after.'

All the time thinking that she would slip the letters into the pockets, that the girl would find them, think about them, puzzle it out. She meant to do it the next day, but that was years ago and she had no idea if she really had. And now the girl lived in another country, didn't she? With a husband and dark-eyed children. And who knew what had happened to that fine green coat, what had happened to her shoes, to all those other things she no longer had a use for. The letters could be anywhere or nowhere, but it didn't matter in the same way; she realized that she had let them go, sometime, without even noticing. And she thought how it seemed to get easier and easier as you got older, this unburdening. When she had moved to an apartment from the old house her sons had minded, her grandchildren more, but she herself had not felt a thing, closing the heavy front door.

Her husband had a kind face, a small moustache. When he asked if he might see her again there was something in his voice, his eyes, that said that it would be a serious business. The girl she had been would have run from that, to a dance or a stroll by the lake. A few years before she would have told him no and moved on without pause, as if the question had nothing at all to do with her. But a few years before the people she loved

were all still alive. Her mother and father, Beattie and Archie
and Tom.

She had always thought Archie a bit of a fool, just one of the
boys singing silly songs on someone's veranda. But then he died
in the mud with her picture in his pocket, and she thought that
she might have loved him. And then Beattie with the baby in
her arms, and Tom so soon after. Her mother dropped a cup in
the kitchen; it fell so slowly that Amelia could see every shift,
every half-turn in the air, a few drops of tea spinning out like
something much thicker. Her mother knew from that moment
and when they finally came to tell her she only nodded, caught
her breath with one jagged, tearing sound.

Tom's last letter came the next day, like something out of a
dream. *My dearest little sister,* he wrote, *for you will always be
that to me....* Going on to tell her  the usual things about his
strange routine, the noise of the big guns. At the end of the letter he told her not to worry so much, that he had this feeling
that he would be all right. She was astonished that he could be
so wrong.

Hugh went to war too; he lived, but did not come back. It
seemed that she had known him forever, known him since he
and Tom were inseparable, going off on mysterious journeys
with willow whips in their hands and their caps askew. Chas-
ing her away when she tried to follow. She was wild in those
days, climbing to the tops of trees. Her hair a tangle and her
stockings always torn, her mother's despair. The boys teased
her terribly and once in a rage she threw a tin shovel that
caught Hugh near the eye, making him bleed. His face went
pale but he didn't make a sound, just turned and walked carefully back to the house where her mother and Ada clucked and
patched him. Amelia sent to her room for the rest of the day,
watching the changing light in a stupor of fear and shame.

Hugh lived with an old aunt, a parson's widow who was
always trying to beat the Lord into him. Or so Tom said, and it

may have been true; he was always at their house, and their father didn't seem to mind. Teased him and gave him chores to do, just like Tom, and lectured him too when they'd been caught at something. Like the time they rigged a bucket of kitchen slops in the pear tree over the swing, soaking Beattie and her new beau. Poor Beattie had been so furious, the three of them listening outside the door to her loud voice, and their father's. But that must have been another time, Beattie wailing that she would die, just die if she couldn't be with Jack. So she married him, after all those battles, and then she died anyway. And because of him, some might say, for how could you blame a tiny baby that barely drew breath. He married again, Beattie's Handsome Jack, and for a long time he marched in the parade once a year. Growing fatter and fatter — who would have thought? With a big red nose and his empty sleeve pinned tight.

When she was a little older Amelia sometimes went with Tom and Hugh on their jaunts about the town, and they took her to the fair once, holding both her hands. Already they were starting to become themselves, with Tom the one who worried. Would she be sick on the carousel, frightened by the Monkey Boy. Maybe not knowing that nothing could harm her while he was standing there.

Hugh didn't worry; he grew up careless with a way of making people laugh even while they were telling him that one day he would go too far. That day at the station he made it seem like the greatest adventure, even his aunt was smiling in her musty dress, smelling like some kind of tonic. He and Tom hanging out the train window while they all blew kisses and waved their flags.

When Hugh did come back it was ten years later; she opened the door one afternoon and knew him immediately. Behind him a soft rain was falling and when he swept off his hat in the doorway tiny droplets scattered like a handful of flung stars.

She made tea and they talked about the old house, the old days, the flu that took her parents and so many others. Her sons woke, bright-eyed and ravenous, and Hugh took off his vest and rolled around on the floor with them, Thomas and Stephen bringing out all their treasures and making a terrible mess, grinding crumbs into the carpet. While she just laughed and laughed.

Over dinner her husband asked Hugh about his work, his travels. He had been everywhere, it seemed, and was just then with a mining company in South America. Her husband knew something about engineering from his work with the city and she drifted in and out of their technical talk, feeling light enough to float away. Thinking how strange it was that Hugh should be there, looking just the same. Looking even more like himself, somehow; everything a little thicker, more solid around the edges. But still with that twitching smile, the way he rubbed his thumb under his chin while he listened to someone. The nick near the corner of his eye that was scarcely visible, even if you knew to look for it.

She wondered sometimes what her husband had thought, what he had known or seen. When he was dying for so long he forgot things, and he liked her to sit by the bed and remind him. *What did we call that dog we had, not Sadie but the other one, the one with the white tail. What was that pie you made, that I used to like so much. What was the name of that fellow that came, the one that made you laugh....* And then he was silent, and she didn't know what he was thinking.

How long did Hugh stay — a week? A month? She had no idea, only knew that he came to see her almost every day, that she was easy in his company, in the way he knew things about her that no one else did, because they were things she would never think to mention. The doll that she carried under her right arm until she went to school, its drooping eye. The way she hid herself in the branches of trees for hours at a time, the way she wore her hair at sixteen.

Her housework suffered terribly as the weather grew warmer; they took the boys for long walks through the parks, down to the lake, and sometimes Hugh hired a car and they had picnics in the country. Once they went to see Ada, who lived in a tiny house with her younger sister. She was a little frail, a little muddled about things; she thought they had married each other and kept saying how kind they were, bringing their fine sons to visit. Telling the boys in a high, thin voice what scamps their parents had been, when they were young.

Walking home, Hugh said it was all like a dream. Coming back and seeing places, people looking just the same, and yet not quite. 'You, for instance,' he said, 'you have a look of Tom when you're serious, that I don't remember from before.'

And then he told her that he'd had malaria, that it came back from time to time. And he told her that once he'd seen her face in a delirium, but she didn't believe him for a minute. That kind of talk came as easily to Hugh as breathing and didn't she use to hear them, him and Tom, lounging under the pear tree, talking about the kind of nonsense girls liked to hear. 'No — no, it's true,' Hugh said, and she found herself wondering.

Another time, lying on his back on a rough picnic blanket, Hugh told her what she had often wondered — that he hadn't been there when Tom died. And because she asked him, he told her some things about how it was in that place, how some men shot off feet or hands, maimed themselves in all kinds of ways, just to get out of it. Watching the clouds in the sky he told her things so terrible she couldn't have begun to imagine them, and she knew that even these were not the worst things. And then suddenly he jumped up, roaring like a fierce tiger, and chased Thomas and Stephen over the green grass until they all fell down, laughing.

Other times he talked about places he'd seen in the world, and he told her about Bolivia, where the new mine was. How the stars were much brighter there, and the moon too. The smell of the air. He described the costume he wore, riding through the hills. Baggy trousers and a wide-brimmed hat. His horse splashing through streams where native women bathed. 'You should see it,' he said, 'you should come out there, sometime.'

And she said that she would like to and he said that she could come back with him and she laughed and said of course she could, nothing to it. And they joked about it after that, playing it like a game from years before. The journey by boat, by train, by cart. The house he would build and what she would see, looking out each window. The food they would eat, the chickens and the cow in the yard. How every few months they would travel to a city, put on fine clothes and walk among the people, and how after a day they would long to be away again. They played the game over and over until she could really see herself, standing in the sunshine or riding out to meet him on a horse named Blaze.

Hugh stayed a week or a month and then he came to say goodbye, bringing presents for the boys to find when they woke. It was a warm spring night; her husband was not at home and they sat on the old swing on the back porch, drinking something cool and looking out at the dark garden. Once she thought she heard a child cry out, but upstairs her sons were fast asleep. When she turned from touching a cheek he was there in the doorway, a dark shadow glowing with light at the edges, and it was like a moment she had always known would come. He held on to her wrist very tightly as they walked back down the stairs, back through the kitchen where striped towels dried on the rack, back to the porch, the empty glasses, the swing. 'Come with me,' Hugh said. 'You must come with me.'

In the letters Hugh wrote things to hurt her, and they did hurt her. Things about life in the camp, about the dances they had at the end of the week, the makeshift lanterns and the wildness. How the women of that country, when beautiful, were very beautiful.

Around the hurtful things he wrote others. Details of his life, his work, and talk about their friendship, how much it would always mean to him. She knew Hugh, knew his boyhood swagger and the look of his back, walking away. And so she read his letters, and wrote her own. Little things that were happening in the city. The birth of her third son.

She had always thought that Raymond was somehow Hugh's child. Impossible, of course, but there was a kind of life in him always, a recklessness and a careless joy that often made her catch her breath. Even the way he died — the full moon, the fast car — was so exactly what he would have chosen that in the midst of all her pain the person she longed to tell was Hugh.

But by then the letters had stopped, and she had gotten used to that. Would maybe have forgotten them completely, except for that way he always had of sneaking up on a person. Leaping out from behind bushes and doorways when they were children, making her scream and clasp her heart. She continued to be ambushed all her life, the brush catching in her hair as the thought of him appeared, the light catching his cheek in a certain way. Or sometimes as she never had seen him, in baggy trousers and a wide-brimmed hat, splashing through clear water.

If I am old, she thought, then Hugh is that much older. Or maybe dead — there was no one left who would tell her that, if they happened to hear of it. No one left who would even remember if she had opened the door one afternoon and found him standing there. He could have died in an accident years ago, or from malaria or some other thing. But it seemed to her that if he had died she would have known, or remembered.

She wondered if it was the same for Hugh; she had often wondered that. It had seemed an easy decision to make, at first

— hardly a decision at all. Watching the daylight come into her house, the solid feel of it, of the place where she was. If she had still been that wild-haired girl, dancing through the tops of trees, it would have been a different matter. But lying in her high bed she knew that girl was gone gone gone, drawn down long ago by the weight of the earth all around.

The next day her arms were streaked with flour and there were people coming to dinner; she watched Hugh walk away with something like relief, turning back to her own front door. And it was only later, raising a spoonful of fruit to her lips, that she began to feel the pain. To ask herself why it couldn't be true that she loved him, had always loved him, that his shadow in the doorway was the one moment it had all been leading to, and from.

So she wondered if it was the same for Hugh, or if it had just been a moment for him. A flicker of memory, the scent of lilacs in a room that was warm with the breath of sleeping children. All the things that made it impossible for her to go. People did, of course; women did. In the dark and terrible time that followed she heard about them everywhere. In the newspaper, around dinner tables, at the grocer's counter. Ordinary women who left home and family, who gave up everything, for love. She showed herself no mercy then.

But there had been no surprise in Hugh's face when she told him, and thinking of that she told herself that he hadn't been serious, that he knew very well the solid feel of her house, the way her sons held each hand, anchoring her to the ground. That he wouldn't have asked if he'd thought for a minute that she would shake herself free and sail away beside him. She told herself that over all the things she knew, and made herself believe it. Almost believe it. An old woman still wondering — what if she had changed her mind? Had followed by the next boat, had found him on some dusty track. Would he have been delighted, or appalled?

She wondered now if Hugh was the thing for her life, if there was one thing for everyone's life. A thing that kept coming around and around, a thing that stayed to the end. And then suddenly she thought that she'd got it all wrong; she remembered those women she'd admired in the newspaper and wondered if they'd had it mixed up too. When Hugh tightened his fingers on the base of her thumb it gave a form to things, but perhaps the real thing that took the shape of Hugh was more complex, the yearning for something else entirely. And she thought that it was such a waste, the way you started to figure things out so late. The way the knowing wasn't anything you could pass on anyway.

The way it was now, it was all coming and going. She remembered a high window, she remembered her small white bed and a time when she had longed for sleep, had longed for the dreams to start. The thought that there was this other life going on that was hers too, but so different. Sometimes now she was aware of sinking back with just that sense of anticipation. And sometimes she wasn't aware of it at all. Sometimes she heard her name, and hearing it realized that it had been going on for a long time, drawing her back so slowly from wherever she happened to be. Sometimes then she saw a face, almost familiar, or maybe a soft blur of pastel. And sometimes nothing but the long window, a view of tall buildings, small oblongs of sky in darkening shades. Who would choose to stay there?

That day at the fair the sky was blue and her hands were sticky, held tight by Tom and Hugh. Her heart was thumping as if it would burst and inside her skin it was all dancing, leaping, and there was music playing, voices and wonderful hot smells. They set her on a painted horse and she held tight to the pole as it began to go up and down and around and around and she had never been so happy. And each time around she saw Tom and Hugh watching her from the side, their arms about each other's shoulders and their caps tipped back, their smiling faces. The blue sky behind them and all the people and the wonderful hot smells and the *tap-tap* of the merry-go-round.

And then once around they weren't there, an empty space, the scuffed brown grass where they had been standing and she whipped her head around, her long hair flying and panic rising but then they were back again and it was all right and she thought she saw Archie standing near them, his chipped tooth and his foolish freckles. She held tight to the pole and rested her cheek, the light touch on her lower lip, and there were so many people and this time around there was someone with the look of Beattie, holding a baby and pointing, and her mother's hand with the thin gold band, tucked into the crook of her father's arm. Around and around and she thought, What a long ride, and she had never been so happy, going faster and faster around and around and her husband's kind eyes and Raymond with something sticky on his chin and faster and faster and Hugh laughing and all the bright stars of Bolivia and she wondered if she would go on spinning like this forever —

# Maya

The summer she was almost thirteen her mother married a tall man and went on a long tour of America. And it seemed that everyone on the kibbutz wanted to tell her how wonderful it all was, the best thing that could have happened. She knew all that, of course she knew it. And if the whole thing took her by surprise at first, well, that was only because she hadn't really been paying attention. She thought that she'd been noticing her own difference, something to do with the way her face seemed to be changing, the way her whole body seemed to ache and itch and betray her. But when her mother told her, on a windy afternoon when the winter rains had stopped, then everything rearranged itself, snapped into a new place. Through the window there were white clouds and cool wind-tossed trees and as her mother began to speak, Maya remembered everything. The voices of women over cups of coffee, a tone to their laughter. There was a pause, no longer than an indrawn breath, while the pieces of the new picture nudged and curled around each other. And in that pause, as thick tears began to form, she pushed them down, telling herself that it was all her fault, that if only she had paid *attention*. If only she had kept her mind fixed on the way things were, they would have stayed forever.

All through the spring people told her how wonderful it all was, and Maya said, *I know, of course I know*. But they wouldn't stop, kept on talking into summer, talking as if she were a child about to make a scene, stamp her feet and throw things at the wall. Sewing her up with their soft sliding words, leaving no space for anything to leap out. While her mother fastened her seat belt and flew away to America, holding the hand of the tall man who would always sit beside her.

They left a map behind; America was a jagged red line

crawling through cities with whispering names, touching several seas before it closed itself in. For days Maya waited for a message, for a call that would say, Come with me, come now, whatever was I thinking of, leaving you behind. But there were only postcards, telling how everything was new and strange and wonderful. Chicago was a street like a canyon, a line of brightly painted cars. Her mother wrote, *Gal keeps falling down, he tips his head back, trying to see the sky.* Gal's letters cut in with thick, broad strokes; he wrote, *Not true, your mother is dreaming again.* Sometimes four or five cards arrived at once and Maya laid them out through the long afternoons, trying to match the red line of America. I should tell her to write the date, she thought, so I would know. But her mother was gliding across America and there was no place to send a letter, no way to tell her anything.

The summer she was almost thirteen sprinklers hissed under a taut blue sky, and everything seemed to have slipped somehow sideways, beyond control. Maya trailed hot fingers through water, through the droning afternoons, while everyone slept behind shuttered windows. Lying by the swimming pool she squeezed her eyes shut, tightly, trying to catch hold of things. School was finished and her class worked four hours every day and already people knew that she couldn't find her place. Out in the fields she fainted under the pulsing sun, and the nurses pressed cool palms to her forehead and promised to arrange inside work. But in the laundry the clothes she pulled from machines were streaked and speckled, and in the dining room breakable objects leapt from her hands, leaving her near tears in a room littered with shards of glass and jagged-edged plates. She was terrified of the cows and too slow in the factory, and the babies screamed at her touch. All she wanted was to move silently, invisibly through the summer, but things kept sliding sideways, slipping from one bad thing to a worse one, and she knew that she was becoming a problem, discussed in the work organizer's office, discussed over coffee by all her mother's friends. Every night she said, Tomorrow it will be all right, tomorrow everything will be back in its place. But she slept late in the mornings, waking cloudy and panicked, saying, Not again, oh no, not again. Running to the main kitchen where they wrapped her in an apron, gave her a knife and a pail and left her on a stool in the corner, digging the eyes from potatoes. Steam pots hissed and clattered and voices slashed through the air; knife blades flashed and the women moved with a slow, shuffling walk over a floor made slick and dangerous with the slimy pulp of discarded vegetables. Later, they killed fish. Fresh from the ponds, black-eyed and struggling, big as a grown man's arm. When Maya slipped and fell painfully down, a bucket tipped and severed heads rolled about her body. Old women clucked their tongues as they brushed the hair from her eyes, poked and prodded at her bones. Their voices were kind but their hands were streaked with blood. Fish scales clung to their cheeks, glinted in their eyebrows, and she prayed that she was dreaming and would wake up soon.

This is the worst, Maya thought, climbing the steps to the work organizer's office. Stepping sideways as Fat Ziva slammed through the screen door, calling over her shoulder, *Enough is enough, I've done my share, more than — do you hear what I say?*

Tomorrow will be all right, Maya thought, sitting on the edge of a square wooden chair, still warm from Fat Ziva's agitated weight. The walls of the office were papered with charts, red arrows linking names and places, and a slow-turning fan lifted the scraps of paper that littered the work organizer's desk, breezed across Maya's face as she said, *Anything else, I'll do anything else, but I can't go back there. All right,* the work organizer said, *all right.* Writing her name in square red letters and linking it to another with a carefully drawn line. And as Maya closed the door, standing again in the flowered sunlight, she saw that she'd been moving on that line all along.

Bouncing from bad to worse, but really moving along a line
that led right to Vered.

Vered had glittering eyes and a terrible slow disease. A disease
like a hand, squeezing tighter and tighter, twisting her limbs
and hunching her shrunken body, squeezing all the rage that
one person could contain in a hard, pure mass. Doctors had
shuffled through papers and said she'd be dead by twenty-five,
but rage pushed her on through the years, twice that. For a long
time she moved with crutches, smashing them down on the
dusty paths. First one, then the other, dragging her twisted legs
between. She left a trail of concentric circles pressed in the silky
dust and the children followed it, moving silently, close to the
ground. Always afraid that they would come across her lurching shadow, just beyond the next clump of bushes. For years
Vered ranged all over the kibbutz, stamping her angry, even
circles, ending always at her own room, throwing herself down
on her own hard bed. Until one day she fell and could not get
back up, lay for hours out near the swimming pool because she
wouldn't call for help. They bought her a wheelchair, electric,
and the children ran from the whine of the motor.

Vered fought with everyone and it grew worse as she aged,
needing more and more tending, sinking farther into herself.
The women took turns bringing her food, cleaning her room,
and she drove them away, one by one, always finding the exact
spot, secret and defenceless. Young women who loved their
husbands and lived in a warm, milky dream; older women who
had known the worst of times. Even Fat Ziva, who remembered
a white room, a skinny girl sitting on a wooden chair while a
doctor shuffled through papers. She was discussed in committee rooms, endlessly, and people were sent to talk to her. They
talked sternly, reasonably, and in the end they threatened. *We'll
have to send you away*, they said, *to some institution. This
can't go on*, they said, *you have to try. You'll end up alone in
your room with no one to help you, is that what you want?*

*That won't happen*, Vered said, *that will never happen. And you won't send me away, do you think I'm a fool? Of course you won't send me away.*

And she was right, no one could quite decide to do it. *We've managed this long*, they said in the committee rooms, *we can carry on a little longer; it can't be much longer.* They'd been saying it for years. And all the time Vered sat hunched in her room, curled around her hate. Polishing it smooth as it grew like some slow pearl, pure and hard and bright enough to blind you.

All night Maya writhed and kicked, lost in a dream like a canyon, with strange eyes peering from a thousand dark crevices. But the morning came anyway, the sun high and cruel at eight o'clock, each leaf standing clear and sharply etched. Most people had been up for hours, loud voices calling to each other as they slapped red dust from their clothes, scrubbed hands outside the dining room. Maya walked away into silence, carrying a tray of food. Bread and creamed cheese, a cucumber, carrot. A blood-red tomato and a jug of strong, sweet tea. The metal jug nudged the heavy plate with a tiny, clean sound as she walked past explosions of bougainvillea. Past the tangled rosebushes, white and red, and up a ramp that led to a shuttered door. A voice croaked and she opened the door into darkness, stood blinded, blinking, while the morning light blazed behind her. The voice said, 'Why do I have an air conditioner if idiots keep holding my door open?' and she closed it quickly, making the dishes dance.

'Be *careful*,' the voice said, 'you'll spill it, clumsy girl. Put it here, on the table.'

Vered sat in a low armchair, inspecting the tray. All tangled hair and sharp angles, prodding the food with a twisted, bony finger. The main room was bare and very clean. A small couch, table, a neat stack of magazines. One rose in a tall vase, and on the wall a child's drawing of a clown, framed and faded.

'Are you deaf, girl?' Vered said. 'I'm talking to you. Who are you, that's what I want to know.'

'I'm Maya,' Maya said. 'I'm Lili's daughter. And Amram's.'

'Amram's dead,' Vered said. 'He's been dead for years.'

'I know,' Maya said.

'And Lili ran off to America with some man, I heard. I hear things.

'Well, at least you know how to knock,' Vered said. 'Not like that fat Ziva, walking right in as if it was her own house. Cow. I told her, I said, You should have learned your lesson years ago, walking into your sister's house and finding your husband just putting his shirt on. She didn't like that, not one bit.

'The bread's stale,' Vered said.

'I'm sorry,' Maya said. 'Do you want me to cut things for you?'

'I'm not helpless,' Vered said, clenching a fist around the heavy knife. 'I'm not a child.'

The knife crashed against the plate as she hacked at the food and finally she threw it to the floor, shouting, 'Stupid girl, what's wrong with you? A dull knife like that won't cut anything.'

'I'm sorry,' Maya said. 'I'll do it.'

The tomato burst as the knife touched it, red juice and seeds dripping from the edge of a thick white plate, and Maya thought, I was right, this is the worst, this has got to be the worst thing.

Vered ate greedily, scattering bits of food, ripping at the bread with sharp white teeth. Maya opened the shutters and sunlight slashed across the room, tearing a curled petal from the rose in the narrow white vase.

'So Lili ran off to America and left you behind,' Vered said. 'Didn't want you around to spoil the fun, I guess.'

Maya walked carefully, carrying the dishes into the tiny kitchen, but the voice went with her.

'I know that Lili,' it said, 'always thinking of herself.

Probably sends you pretty postcards, doesn't she,' the voice
said, as Maya turned the taps on full. 'Says, Oh how I miss you,
wish you were here. Ha. If that's what she wanted she would
have taken you. Right? Girl, am I right?'

I just won't listen, Maya said. I will wash the dishes and I
will wash the floor and I will do whatever she wants, but I just
won't listen.

At the swimming pool Shula said, 'Don't go back, just say that
you won't go back,' and Hanna said, 'No one can *make* you go
back.'

But when Maya said, 'Where else can I go?' they didn't
answer.

She stared down at their distorted feet, moving slowly
through warm water; Shula and Hanna worked in the fields
and their limbs were dusky and strong, nudging against Maya's
pale legs from either side.

'You tell me,' she said, 'you tell me, where else can I go?'

'Then just ignore her,' Hanna said, as a blond boy jumped
from the high board, spraying them with sparkling water.

'What can she do to you?' Hanna said. 'She can't *do* anything.'

And Shula nudged from the other side and said, 'Hanna's
got a secret, ask Hanna about her secret,' and Hanna said,
'Don't you tell, Shula, you promised you wouldn't tell.'

They began to giggle and splash at each other, grabbing
hands and rolling into the water on the curve of their laughter.
Maya watched them wriggling side by side beneath the surface,
sleek and brown and strong. Walking home through the blazing
centre of the afternoon she felt her white body swelling, and
wondered how so many things could change, just because she
stopped paying attention.

Later a hot wind clattered through palm trees and stroked
the flaming flowers as Maya walked to the room of her mother's
friend, sat on the floor watching the baby pound thick wooden

pegs into a board filled with holes. The other children watched television, enthralled. A man with a clown's white face, drooping mouth, did magic tricks, producing scarves, eggs, flowers, from his hat, from his pockets, from the sleeves of his multi-coloured coat.

'You can't let her upset you, that's all,' Ruti said, lighting a cigarette, walking into the next room to find a cracked blue ashtray.

'Just remember that she's old and sick and tells lies, and sometimes she says terrible things, trying to make you angry.

'Just don't pay any attention to her,' Ruti said, turning ash from the end of the cigarette. 'I know, I've had my turn, that's the only way.'

The children shrieked with laughter; a sudden strange look on the clown's face as objects begin to appear, sprouting from sleeves, cuffs, from hidden pockets everywhere. Large astonishment on his face as he slaps at his body, snatching at flowers appearing faster and faster, throwing them to the floor, throwing them away, only to find the next bunch nudging into sight from a pocket near his heart.

'But *why* do I have to do it,' Maya said. 'Why do *I* have to do it?'

'It's nothing to do with you,' Ruti said. 'Nothing *personal*, it's just the way things are. We all have to do things we don't want to sometimes, you know that. That's just how it is.'

'Remember,' Ruti said, getting up to turn off the television, 'remember, it's only for a week or two, until they find someone else; it's not like it's forever. Just don't let her upset you, just don't listen to what she says.'


'They took out all my organs,' Vered said, while Maya straightened the covers on the hard bed. 'Oh, I had boyfriends, lots of them, you can be sure of that. And all the young soldiers. The women didn't like it, they were jealous, all of them, but it didn't matter. You'd be surprised, you would, all the men who came to my room at night. But then they took out all my organs. It's for the pain, they said, it's so you won't have to have that pain. Liars.'

Maya filled an orange pail with warm water, soap. Her father was a boy soldier, framed and hanging on the wall beside her bed. His khaki shirt was streaked and crumpled and his face was slightly blurred, caught in the act of turning away.

'Do you have boyfriends, girl?' Vered said. 'Where do you go with the boys at night, what do you do with the boys at night?'

'I don't go anywhere,' Maya said, soaking a striped cloth in warm water. 'I don't do anything.'

'They took everything out so I couldn't have children,' Vered said. 'Did you know that? Nobody would marry me, knowing I couldn't have children. Who would marry me, knowing a thing like that. Tell me, who?'

'I don't know,' Maya said.

'Stupid girl,' Vered said. 'Nobody, that's who.'

Every morning Maya carried a tray of food past the twisted rosebushes. She washed the dishes, she washed the clean floor, she placed a white rose in a narrow vase and opened the shutters, watching Vered wince as the sunlight slapped her eyes, picked out flecks of white cheese clinging to the corners of her mouth. She helped Vered move from chair to chair, slipping her hands into the jagged hollows under her arms, saying each time, You're nothing but an old bag of bones, you can't hurt me, you're just an old bag of bones.

'It's not so bad,' she told Ruti. 'She talks and talks but I just don't listen.'

And Ruti smiled, shifting the weight of the baby in her arms, and said, 'Yoash told me that he offered to change you. That you wanted to stay.'

'Well, I'm used to it now,' Maya said. 'The summer's almost over, and it's really not so bad.'

But all night she wandered through dream canyons, where voices whispered from dark shadows and the real world seemed to be gone forever. In the morning the floor was cool beneath her feet and she shut the door quickly, making the dishes dance. Vered sat in her wheelchair, cradling a sheaf of wild roses in her bony lap. Stray leaves and petals whispered along the floor; shears glinted in a dark corner. And the room lurched as Maya set the tray down, pieces of the picture beginning to shudder, to inch apart.

'You're late,' Vered said. 'Lazy girl — I picked these hours ago. Here, take them, put them in something.'

She held out the bundle, and as Maya took it something bit into her finger, making her cry out. In the kitchen she saw the thorn, only one, dark and wickedly curved. Oh, she said, rocking slowly as dark blood dripped into the cracked white sink. Oh oh oh oh oh.

The postcards still came, almost every day; city streets and brightly coloured cars, the lights of Las Vegas dancing against a purpled sky.

Walking beneath tall trees Maya told herself that the circle of America was almost closed, but the words were faint and far away. Fat Ziva pinched her cheek between thick fingers and said, 'Girl, you have such patience, I don't know how you do it. You really have made some connection, everyone says so.'

Maya knew what they were saying, knew what it meant when the old women smiled and patted her head as she walked by. And sometimes she thought that it might be true; sometimes, outside, it seemed that it might even be true. But inside the dark room she knew better. The disease was a slow hand, squeezing now at Vered's throat, and in the mornings her voice was garbled, harsh as a rusty can. But as the sun pulsed hotter, the words began to slither and flow. Some days she spoke of all her lost children, the revenge of jealous women. Pilfering small objects and leaving the floor streaked with dirt, taking advantage. But mostly she spoke of secret lives, of shapes she saw rolling in the long dark grass. Vered didn't sleep, she said that she didn't sleep; said that she sat all night at her darkened window, watching. People in forbidden places, echoes of the soft footsteps that crept to her door, before she couldn't have children. Even Amram, she said, had stroked her withered thighs. While his wife slept. While his wife played her whore's game with every man around. Outside, these things all seemed to be lies. But in Vered's room they flowed like gently bubbling oil, flowed over Maya, bringing warmth to a place that was hollow and cold, the summer she was almost thirteen.

Bag of bones, Maya said softly, sweeping a wet cloth across the floor in steadily increasing arcs. I hate you, Maya crooned softly, hate hate hate you.

When the summer was almost over, the health committee hired a deaf woman from the town to care for Vered. *It's the next best thing*, they said. *Why didn't we think of it years ago.* The deaf woman rode the early bus every morning, speaking cheery hellos with her darting fingers. Vered's mouth opened and closed, but she paid no attention. She washed the dishes, she washed the clean floor, and only smiled, from time to time, at the shrunken figure in the low armchair.

And Maya came out of a dark dream, waking late one morning and feeling, suddenly, that everything was back in its place. She lay by the swimming pool with Shula and Hanna, trailing brown fingers while the sun stroked their bodies. Telling secrets, all of them, wriggling beneath the green water and breaking the surface together, laughing and flinging careless drops from their hair. She walked home beneath tall moving trees and slept away the long afternoons in a cool room, while filtered sunlight danced on the ceiling. She helped Ruti clean her mother's room, sweeping up the dust of the summer, putting fresh sheets on the bed and fresh flowers in a vase of sparkling crystal. And early one morning she rode with Ruti to Tel Aviv, stood behind smudged glass in an airport filled with voices and was suddenly in her mother's arms, breathing in the smell of America while her mother said, 'You've got so tall, when did you get so tall? I was so excited I couldn't sleep at all, just ask Gal, not a wink!'

All of them laughing and talking, collecting suitcases and bags and driving along the coast road with the windows down, wind whipping their hair, because her mother was longing for the smell of that sea. Laughing and talking and her mother ripping through brightly coloured bags, plastic snapping in the wind of their travelling, bringing out shirts and skirts and sunglasses, piling them in Maya's lap, saying, 'Do you like this, do you really? When I saw it I knew it would be perfect, I just knew it.'

Maya sat hunched in the back seat, wedged between her laughing mother and sharp-cornered cases as the smell of America faded out into the smell of the blue sea. Sucking at a scratch on her finger, saying, It's all right now, it has to be all right now. Hunched around something hard and bright, something biding its time, like the seed of a tiny pearl.

# Where You Live Now

Now that you've been dead for weeks instead of days, I find I'm scanning headlines at the checkout once again. Cures for cancer in every issue and Siamese twins delivering each other's babies. A caveman's skull bears an uncanny resemblance to Elvis, who has recently been spotted in Jessup, Georgia. But what makes me stop and stare is a blurred photograph, a story about astronauts finding the footprint of a child on the surface of the moon. It reminds me of that time we sat on the back steps, eating something sticky. How we wondered about the moon, a smudgy print in a hard blue sky, and could it be the same one we saw at night? I thought not.

And then you told me about your favourite aunt, the one with the earrings shaped like broken hearts, the one with the sweet breath. How she'd been driving in her car one day, how she'd driven up the steep hill at the edge of town and ended up in heaven. This did not seem impossible, although I did wonder how she got back.

'Reverse,' you said.


Where I'm living now there are no trees. Dan says I lack imagination; he can look at the spindly things surrounded by hoops of wire and see a forest, in time, lush and overhanging and shading the back patio where he and I will read books in our retirement. I can't even see the back patio, just a churning mass of mud on a pale spring day. The boys love it, of course. They tie faded scarves about their heads and wear their coats like capes; they are superheroes doing constant, complex battle. At times I eavesdrop shamelessly.

That summer there was a strike at the mill and we walked by the

white house on the way to the pool and someone had sprayed
*Scab* in shaky letters all over the side. We couldn't work that out.
And once we stood at the edge of a field; I saw a fat brown slug on
your shoulder, inching its way toward your bare arm. And you
screamed and I screamed and we ran across the whole field and
when we got to the other side it was gone but we took off our
clothes and shook them out, to make sure. After that we always
ran screaming across that field, holding hands.

That summer your brothers made us their slaves, and we
had to get up at six o'clock to do their paper route. They said if
we didn't they would flush us down the toilet and once they
even dragged us down the hall, kicking and shrieking, until
your mother shouted up the stairs. We did the route for a few
days because we both remembered getting stuck when we were
small and the seat was up, how we went right down, just our
calves and shoes kicking above the rim, and how both our
mothers laughed in the doorway before they lifted us out. That
was one of the first bonds between us.

We weren't clever enough to do it on purpose, but we must
have made a terrible mess of the papers because after a few
days your mother started getting calls and you told her the
whole story and when your father came home your brothers got
the belt and lost their allowances for a long time. We thought
we were safe for a little while but sometimes they would sneak
up behind you and make swooshing noises no one else could
hear. Then we were sure they would come for us those times we
slept in the tent in my back yard, but all we heard were the loud
voices going on and on.

And that was the summer my father left and I sacrificed
Becky in the river above the dam. Threw her in and watched
her torn dress billow out, her yarn braids twist and flip as she
was swept along. Now that you're dead there's no one else who
knows how much I cried.

\* \* \*

It was from my mother that I first heard you were sick. She's
retired now; she keeps track of people. In the beginning things
were hopeful and it reminded me, and I thought I would write
you a letter, make some kind of contact, but it was hard after so
much time.

'Oh sure,' I imagined you saying, letting a page flutter
toward the wastebasket.

I did mean to come and see you in the hospital, that last long
time. I got as far as checking the bus schedule, working out the
times so I could make the trip there and back in a day. But
something happened just before I planned to leave, I can't even
remember what, and I never did go. And I thought maybe it
was better that I didn't. I thought maybe it wouldn't help at all
if I came breezing through the door, too much flesh on my
bones and a wallet stuffed with pictures of my sons. I had heard
by then how you longed for a child, how you prayed for a clean
checkup, just one time.

I went to your funeral though, I did manage that. Disguised as
my present self. Your brothers are losing their hair; you knew
that, of course, but I was not prepared. We talked about the
threat of the toilet and laughed, and then they coughed and
touched the corners of their eyes. I didn't show them the pictures I had brought in my purse. You and I on the back steps,
squinting into the sun. And dressed as fairy princesses on
skates for the carnival. During our big number you had to go to
the bathroom and suddenly skated toward the exit. And I, of
course, followed, and so did the other princesses, the frogs, the
teddy bears and the two-person dragon. The music played on
and soft red and green lights bathed the cardboard castle on the
empty ice; our teacher wept with her face in her hands.

Out of nowhere your father decided to go to England for a few
years; you cried and cried but there was no getting out of it. You
came back tall, with an accent I didn't believe for a moment.

Talking about the cinema, the ballet.

'Nothing's changed here,' you kept saying, and I thought I heard my own sneer, grew prickly because of it. Maybe if you'd stayed then we would have found a new place to start from, but you were all living in the city, only coming for a visit once or twice. Talking then about the Third World, talking about becoming a nurse so you could help somewhere. You were only three months older but you grew up so much faster and we let each other go without even noticing. I'd hear things once in a while; you were in Guatemala, in Africa; you were married, then you weren't. But I didn't pay much attention. Years went by when I didn't think of you at all.

Where I live now there are no trees — I think I told you that. I wash the dishes and look out on a sea of mud, my boys now joined by other ragged heroes. They run and jump and fall, soundlessly. I keep waiting for the quiet moments, I keep waiting for the questions I've worked out answers to. If the earth is really spinning, then why aren't we dizzy? If we dig a hole to China, will the people be upside down? Where do you go when you die?

I didn't think I would mind so much, but I keep *remembering*. Twisted red letters on the side of a white house, and Becky tossing in the cold river. That time your aunt cried in the kitchen because she was thirty and your mother gave us money to go to the store. How we sat on the curb and thought that we would never be that old. You weren't.

And I wonder sometimes if you had some inkling, because what I really can't stand is the randomness of it. We stood together at the edge of a field; it smelled like summer and the sun beat down. I was so close that your hair flicked my cheek as you turned your head to see the fat brown slug that inched down your arm, not mine.

On the surface of the moon there is no gravity. No wind, no

rain. The footprint could have been there for thousands of years, undisturbed. But I like to think that it is more recent. I like to think that your child self is dancing there. Or that maybe you touched down briefly, shedding years, on your way to some other place.

# Spanish Grammar

Franco has been dead for a year, and the signs are everywhere. On the sooty sides of buildings and bus shelters, curved round the bumpers of small cars. Even through the café window she sees them, nailed to the trunks of old trees. *Democracia — Sí! Vote Sí!* And here and there a succinct black *No.* If she closes her eyes alternately, she can make them appear, disappear.

*Sí — no — sí — no.*

Stay. Go.

Jaime explained about the referendum once, in a noisy underground bar. 'It's a farce,' he said, 'there has been no education. How can the people make a choice when they don't even understand the question?'

'Pay attention,' Manolo said, from the other side of the table. 'He's right for once, listen to what he says.'

Jaime talks over laughter and crashing glasses and she leans toward his voice; she knows that some kind of history is going on, and she really does want to understand. But while she listens she also watches the way his lips move, forming each word, the way his fingers curve around a squat glass of wine. And she knows that when she tries to remember the conversation, later, these will be the things that have stayed with her.

Manolo shares Jaime's apartment; he studies geography at the university when he is not handing out leaflets on street corners, marching in forbidden places. They never know when he will come slamming through the door, smudges on his face, bruises on his elbows. Bringing them stories of miraculous escapes, racing down alleyways, crawling under parked cars.

'It's a wonderful time to be alive,' he says. 'Possibilities are suddenly in the air. You can almost touch them, taste them.'

He bounces on the edge of the rumpled bed, waving his arms and laughing while Jaime, embarrassed, goes to make coffee.

'You should have seen it,' he says; 'Ay, Jaime,' he calls, 'you should have been there.'

There is a raw scrape above his right eyebrow and cold air rises from his heavy sweater, a faint, smoky smell.

Manolo likes to talk English with her; he claims to have learned it all from old Beatles records.

'I am the walrus,' he says, solemnly. 'A very useful phrase.'

At one time she thought that Jaime might be jealous, a little, of Manolo's quick, slangy English, the way they laugh and laugh together. A certain tension when Jaime appears in the doorway, carrying three cups on a plastic tray.

'Manolo is my friend,' he says, later, when she tries to talk about it. Smooth it.

'Don't you understand anything,' he says, with an anger in his voice that she has not heard before.

'I'm sorry,' she whispers, trying to see his face in the dark. 'I only meant....'

'Don't say it to me,' he says. 'Manolo is the one you have insulted. Don't you know anything?'

Some subtle code of honour that she has crashed right into, with her clumsy American feet.

'Canadian,' she says, automatically. And she falls asleep thinking how silly it is, this argument in loud whispers, in a foreign language.

Jaime claims not to speak English at all, but she knows that is not true. She remembers his accent, the first words he spoke to her.

'It doesn't matter,' he says. 'The point is, that if I were in America — OK, in Canada — I would be speaking English. No?'

She agrees with him, in principle. But it means that she is the one who becomes tangled and lost in the space between words. Shades of meaning.

She closes her eyes, alternately.

The boy waiter brings her another cup of coffee, reaches to empty the ashtray, again. His name is Javier and he has a cousin in Canada; in Montreal, he thinks, or maybe Vancouver. The cousin writes that it is always cold, and that the people are the colour of newspaper.

'Is it true,' Javier says, 'that Canada is covered with snow and ice, that the sun disappears for half the year?'

He doesn't seem to believe her answer, asks the same thing each time he sees her, as if hoping that she'll let the truth slip out.

The café is owned by Javier's uncle, who is not really his uncle, but a good friend of his father. The tables lean a little and the floor is scattered with bits of paper, cigarettes, but it is nearly empty in the afternoons, and if the uncle's back is turned Javier sometimes brings her a free cup of coffee, a small glass of brandy. He is almost fourteen and already an outrageous flatterer, praising her accent, her vocabulary, her eyes. He can't believe that she learned it all in school, says that he, for example, didn't learn a single thing, when he used to go to school.

Between customers Javier washes dishes behind the counter, watching himself in the misty mirror that also reflects the leaning tables, the door. Takes out a white comb and passes it through his hair, smoothing the wake with his left hand. There is a tight swagger in his walk that tells her that in another year or two he will be unbearable, lounging around fountains, clicking his tongue and calling out after all the girls. But in the meantime he is almost fourteen, and amazed by his own reflection. Still wanting to hear about a place where people live beneath the snow, at the dark end of the world.

The café table is scattered with books and papers. A map of the city and a blue pad with a rising airplane on the cover. Two postcards, a newspaper, a thick red notebook and a text of Spanish grammar. She has been trying to write a letter, but the pen lies abandoned across a flimsy blue page. *Still here*, it says, *although the weather's getting colder*. And something about the rain, how it drips down through the wet yellow trees in all the parks in the city.

In the first weeks, she was determined to do it right. She left the apartment early, collected maps and guidebooks and walked the crisp blue city for hours. Plaza Mayor, Plaza Canovas, Puerta del Sol. She bought the textbook, notebook, a black pen, and produced new phrases for Jaime, in the evenings. He was pleased, but mostly amused.

'I thought you were on holiday,' he said, 'what are you doing, working so hard?'

'Come over here,' he said, 'you speak well enough already.'

*Translate into Spanish: What do you want?*
*Translate into English: Es necesario comprender todo.*

She still goes out each day, though not so early. Walks through twisting familiar streets until she reaches the Gran Via. Walks through the park, around and around, stopping by the grey waters of the artificial lake. When it rains, she follows tour groups in the Prado, sits on a wooden bench in front of a dark painting of a royal family. Some days she spends hours in the café across from the park, completing exercises, copying sentences in the red notebook. The things she reads often astound her. Past Contrary-to-Fact Conditions. Present Unreal Conditions. The significance of the subjunctive mood.

* * *

*Translate: Tengo hambre. Tengo frío. Tengo dolor.*
*I am hungry. I am cold. I have pain.*

'What did you do today,' Jaime says, as the streetlights flicker on. And sometimes she says, 'Waited for you,' because sometimes it is true. But she always laughs when she says it, giving him a choice.

*In the Spanish language the verb* esperar *means both to wait and to hope: meaning must therefore be determined by context.*

She meets Jaime near his office, in the evenings, and they make their way through crowded streets, through brightly lit bars, thick with cigarette smoke and laughter. Wine in heavy tumblers and long glass cases displaying various dead things. Something that looks like kite string, wrapped around a cross of wood.

'What is that,' she says, and when she doesn't recognize the word, Jaime points to his stomach, making signs.

'*Intestines?*' she says, and he laughs at her squeamishness.

'Try this,' he says, touching different delicacies to her lips.

'Open,' he says, 'open.'

And she does.

Often Manolo is with them, at the beginning of the evening. On his way to a meeting, on his way to paint signs or, more rarely, to study. They are always in motion, sampling tapas here and there, a meal somewhere else, coffee. Meeting Jaime's friends everywhere, in bars and restaurants, in front of shop windows. Everyone wants to touch him; the men slap his back, punch his shoulder, and the women rest their hands on his as he bends to light their cigarettes. She sees now how rare it was, in the summer. Lying on a beach in the south with their little fingers resting side by side.

'We don't have to go out every night,' she says. 'You don't have to entertain me.'

But he says, 'It's the way I live. Whether you are here or not.'

It seems to be true; his apartment is clean and bare, a place to shower and sleep, occasionally make coffee. If Manolo is home, they never make love.

'Very quietly,' she whispers, but he whispers that it wouldn't be polite. He would prefer to live alone, if only he could afford it. Most of his money goes to Barcelona, to his wife and son.

'Divorce is not so easy,' he says. 'And anyway, my son would still be my son.'

'You Americans,' he says, stroking her cheek. 'Is that all you're after?'

She has asked herself about that, sitting on a bench, not looking at a picture of a royal family. Thought about how she reads his skin with her fingertips, memorizing clauses, parentheses. Thought about how she watches his profile, driving in the car, how something about it twists right to her heart. There is some secret in the hollow of his temple, the tiny scar near the corner of his eye. Some explanation in the sweep of his lashes that she can't catch hold of, though sometimes it skewers right to her heart.

They go away most weekends, driving and driving to all the places he wants to show her. Toledo, Segovia, San Sebastián. Listening to a tape she bought for him, Bob Dylan singing about simple twists of fate. Or sometimes his own favourite; wild guitar rising, and he raps his thumb on the steering wheel and cries out with Paco de Lucia, *Ay mi alma*. My soul, my soul.

'There's a concert next month,' he says. 'I'll take you, would you like that?'

'If you are still here,' he says.

'If I am still here,' she says.

\* \* \*

*Translate: It is important to know the rules.*

It has always been this way. In darkened rooms they praise each other extravagantly, but in daylight assume little. Like that from the beginning, though perhaps not so obvious. Chance meeting by the sea, in summer. She remembers the sand beneath her bare feet, the weight of the oranges she carried in a paper sack. Moonlight, later, and the soft scent of flowers.

*The past (or imperfect) tense is the most regular and the easiest to form of all the tenses.*

The arrangement allows them to be very kind to each other. They exchange childhoods, produce small treasures from pockets when they meet, in the evening.

'What would you like to do,' Jaime says. 'We'll go anywhere, do anything you like. I only want you to be happy.'

And she believes him. But sometimes at night he makes soft blowing noises in his sleep and she nudges him with an elbow, hard, harder, until he stops. And sometimes it frightens her, how she hits him when he is sleeping, as hard as she can.

Often she knows she made a mistake, following him into real life. Following him a week later, hitching from the south on a straight line, his address on a scrap of paper, growing creased and warm in her clenched hand. Her fingers tremble, she can barely dial the telephone, yet she hears her own voice, casual, saying, 'Well. Hello. Just passing through.'

But she also remembers that he left his office, right away. That he found her in a crowded bar, that he couldn't stop smiling, shaking his head and smiling. These are the things she balances against the apartment where her clothes stay piled on a chair by the door, the women who touch his hands as he bends to light their cigarettes. The look on his face, scanning the room for her. The way he stops and hugs her in the middle of a crowded street, and the way he says her name, sometimes.

Jaime's apartment is small and bare and her clothes stay piled by the door on an old wooden armchair that his wife bought, the first year of their marriage. She is not allowed to answer the telephone; he says that people are following Manolo, that she may be tricked into giving something away. She finds it hard to believe that anyone could think Manolo dangerous, but they both have stories of friends who have been arrested, jailed. One who was shot while disputing a parking ticket.

Some mornings the telephone wakes her, ringing and ringing. She imagines the secret police, blue-jawed and steely-eyed, hunched over the receiver at the other end. Or, more often, Jaime's wife clutching a cigarette between red-tipped fingers, blowing angry puffs of smoke while the telephone rings. Part of the reason that she walks the city all day, although the main part is that she doesn't want him to think that she sits in a chair by a window, waiting for him.

They go away most weekends, driving and driving, and all the places Jaime shows delight her. She is amazed at how he knows his country, knows where to find a tiny, perfect church in a town with dusty streets, knows where to eat chorizo and where to drink cider, poured from a great height. Near Almeria he turns off the main road and shows her where they used to make movies, Western movies. He was an extra once; 'Maybe you saw me,' he says. 'I was an Indian, painted face and feathers in my hair. It was very long then.'

'There were forty of us,' he says, 'riding and whooping. Some of us were supposed to fall off, but I couldn't do it. Held on right to the end.'

'Look at this,' Jaime says, walking through cities, villages, travelling down the coast road with the Mediterranean dancing blue far below.

'Look at this,' Jaime says. 'Remember this.'

But mostly she notices his profile, driving in the car. Or the way sunlight falls on his left hand, resting on a wooden table under a dappling tree.

Sometimes at night they drive through distant towns, looking for a hotel. In the discreet ritual of a Catholic country she waits in the car while Jaime arranges a room. No one wants to see her, although her passport must be examined, recorded. Sometimes in the car she thinks that her passport has checked into hotels all over the country, that Jaime has travelled with her passport all over the country. Hair colour, eyes, the essential data. And a photograph that looks nothing at all like herself.

*Tengo hambre, tengo frío, tengo dolor.*

The thing is, of course, that she is just passing through. On her way to somewhere. Friends are turning brown on the beaches of Greece; postcards arrive, fishermen mending yellow nets under a painful blue sky. She reads the cards in the echoing lobby of the main post office, jostled by brightly coloured backpacks. A murmur of languages seeps around the edges of the lighted telephone cabinas, and she wonders what she is waiting for. Some days, postcard in hand, she begins the long walk to the station to ask about a ticket. But it is a very long walk; she stops for a cup of coffee, along the way. Sees, without warning, the dark planes of Jaime's face as a match flares between his cupped hands.

She thinks then about staying. Manolo says she would have no trouble finding work; people are always looking for tutors, and there is an American school.

'I'll think about it,' she says.

And Jaime says nothing at all.

Sitting in the café across from the park, she asks herself what she is doing. Staying or not staying, looking for answers in the signs nailed to old trees. Reading between the lines of a grammar text. Pushing away the books, the pen, she takes a sip of cooling coffee and smooths out the newspaper. She tries to read it every day, for practice. Tries to guess which stories would catch Jaime's eye, which headlines would make him pause, flipping through.

On this day, it seems that something important has happened. Banner headlines and exclamations, a grainy photograph of a middle-aged man centred on the front page. She remembers that the photograph was visible, in different sizes, on all the newspapers clipped to the side of the kiosk. She assumes that he is dead, but can't quite make it out. Peacefully in his sleep, or in a blinding flash on a street corner; Franco has been dead for a year, and these things happen.

One particular word seems to be the key to the thing, appearing in different forms through all the related articles. *El secuestro, los secuestadores, secuestrar.* Nothing makes sense without this word; she flips through the vocabulary in the back of the textbook, but it isn't there. I should know this, she thinks, trying likely English words. Finding nothing.

'Javier,' she says, calling him away from the mirror, 'Javier, come here a minute. What's this word, what does this word mean?'

'Ah,' Javier says, following her pointing finger. 'Secuestrar. How to explain it? How do you say it — what do you call it, in English, when you catch someone and keep them, when you won't let them go until they have given you what you ask for?'

She tries to tell him, but suddenly she can't stop laughing.

# Archaeology

Now that we are both old I have gone back to school, and this amuses him greatly. At breakfast we watched through the window while the young girls shuffled through fallen leaves, hair in long braids, plaid skirts and thick red knee socks and Benjamin looked from them to me, buttering toast, and said, 'Do you have your pencils sharpened?' Knowing, of course, that I had spent a day in town, preparing. Buying soft-covered note-books, with lines and without, and one with graph paper in a delicate green, different sizes and intensities, for who knows — I might want to study geometry one day. Physics. Choosing felt pens, black and red and three pencils which, yes, I had sharpened. Using a small silver sharpener with a grey smudge in one corner, all that was left of the price tag.

He laughed unfairly for he too knows the seductive power of these objects; we met, in fact, in a stationery shop. I was very impressed by the way he asked for samples of paper, different weights. Rubbed a corner between thumb and finger, held each one up to the light. He said later that he only wanted to keep me near him, to watch me bend, pulling out various packets, the competence in my fingers. This was during his Pre-Raphaelite phase, as I have heard him say many times.

So he is amused, and also annoyed that I am not going about this systematically. It irritates him, the way I take a course here and there, flitting from subject to subject, century to century. 'Why on earth don't you work for a degree?' he says. 'A thing worth doing is worth doing properly,' he says, and I wonder if he hears himself.

There is a pattern, I am dimly beginning to see. Questions answered, needs. I don't expect Benjamin to divine this, don't really want him to, but I am surprised that as a professor of

English literature he should think anything random.

It also annoys him, of course, that I am learning things without his assistance, approval. When I come home he is often reading in his study and he takes off his glasses, says, 'There you are. Well, tell me, what did they say? What did they say about *Alastor*?'

And if it happens to be something he agrees with he will say, 'Yes, yes, but that's putting it a little crudely, you see. It goes so much deeper than that…' Following me out to the kitchen, talking and correcting while I make the tea. He will sometimes admit to this annoyance, flashing a little grin when I least expect it. Benjamin was a poet; he has always been able to acknowledge, disarmingly, most of his faults.

It was not easy at first, armed though I was with my notebooks and pencils, a pile of required and recommended texts. I wrote frantically, trying to take down every word that was said, and in the evenings I transcribed those scribbled notes into another book, neat orderly lines sailing across the page. Benjamin thought it absurd. 'You're only auditing the course, for God's sake,' he said. 'A thing worth doing is worth doing properly,' I said, and he glared at me and left the room. Poor Benjamin, he could have understood if I had volunteered with the Red Cross, would have welcomed me home after the bustle of the annual bake sale. At times it seemed like a better idea. But I carried on, scribbling my way through the first term, and slowly began to understand the language, to understand that I *could* understand the language. That in a course called Marriage and the Family, they really were after the simple answers.

The students took longer to get used to. Some hard, raw edge that I don't remember from my own children with their floating hair and rooms full of incense. In the end I decided that if a boy with green hair and ballet tights found me odd — well, perhaps it was only fair. In the coffee shops and waiting halls I realized that the girls in black with extravagant eyes and twelve

earrings were talking about their broken hearts. That the bril-
liant girl in the philosophy seminar who brought her baby in a
backpack was worried too about what to cook for dinner. Now
we talk between classes, my fellow students and I, and they
often borrow my notes, for my attention to detail has been
observed.

This fall I am taking History of Archaeology, Part I. The
course is taught by a young American woman who wears hik-
ing boots and has only been here a year, and this is a great
relief. There are too many familiar faces, and more than a few
of the professors are former students. It is quite unnerving to
walk into a classroom and see, behind the trim beard and half-
glasses, the face of a pimply boy who once threw up on our living-room carpet.

But this woman, who wants us to call her Gail, has no connection with the more recent past. She lectures well; she has
been on digs all over the Middle East and Central America, and
she makes us feel that we are getting the inside story. In the first
class she talked about the Shanidar cave, the famous Nean-
derthal burials, and I remembered seeing pictures in a maga-
zine, years ago. The uncovering of skeletons: old man, woman,
young man, child. According to the article, pollen samples
showed that at least one had been buried in a flower-lined
grave. Benjamin found me in tears later; I couldn't stop,
couldn't explain. He wrote a poem about it, but there he was
the one who cried.

This week Gail is telling us about Heinrich Schliemann —
the crackpot, she calls him, affectionately; the old fart. His life,
as Gail tells it, unreels like an old movie. The strange young
man surviving shipwrecks, travelling everywhere and master-
ing the languages of the world, amassing great fortunes along
the way. Indulging himself, in middle age, by digging for
fabled Troy. On his way to the site in Turkey he decided that it
was time to marry, and he wrote to the Archbishop of Athens,
asking him to pick out a suitable bride. He was, as Gail says,

characteristically precise. The girl should be young and well educated, with black hair. She should be acquainted with Homer and of the Greek type. If not an orphan, she should at least be poor, forced to eke out a meagre living. As a governess, perhaps. The Archbishop selected a number of candidates and sent the information, along with photographs. And Schliemann fell in love with Sophie's picture.

'Was this the face?' Benjamin said, when I told him my name. And I didn't know Marlowe then but I did know poetry when I heard it, and I thought him daft. But I let him walk me back to the boarding house, wheeling his bicycle through the town, stumbling and knocking into me occasionally. He wore his hair rather long, combed straight back from his forehead, and he ran his fingers through it as he talked.

He talked a lot of rubbish, as I recall, trying to impress me. Which was a bit of a waste because I didn't understand half of it, didn't even really know, for example, what a graduate student *was*. I watched him though, the way he tugged at his hair with his fingers, the rusty bicycle clips that rucked up his pant legs. I remembered how, after all the testing and weighing, he had picked out the cheapest paper in the shop, and how he had paid for it with great dignity, as if it was what he really wanted.

When our children were small Benjamin used to tell them stories about where he grew up. The grand house with servants' quarters in the attic. His father's library, his beautiful mother who played the piano all day. He told the children that his parents had opposed our marriage, that out of loyalty to me he severed all ties with his family. But as I remember it they gave us a silver tea service and invited us to dinner, so they can't have minded that much. The house was large, but not particularly grand, and I don't remember a piano. They talked about their garden, mostly, and about their other son Robert, who was a lawyer in Montreal.

We went to the farm a few times too, in those early years, but

the visits were never successful. I don't know what he had
expected. Landed gentry, perhaps, fallen on hard times but still
with paddocks of fine horses and tea in the afternoon. Or perhaps a quaint little cottage, with chickens scratching delicately
in the yard and my mother knitting by the fire. Not the rambling brick house with no front step. Not the makeshift toilet
and the clammy sheets in the spare room. He thought that my
brothers were savages, not understanding that they were
putting it on a bit. Stamping around in their shit-covered boots,
calling him Ben and asking if he wanted to come help slaughter
a sow. Geld a bull.

He told stories about the farm for years, over dinner tables,
in the faculty club. 'It's incredible,' he would say, 'another
world entirely.' Going on to relate a conversation with a cross-
eyed neighbour, a trip into town to buy rubber boots. Describing corners named for the great cities of Europe where men
mated with their mothers, sister, sheep. Murder, incest, insanity
— to hear him talk you'd think there was a corpse dangling in
every barn in Southwestern Ontario.

But I let him do it, didn't contradict him. I even served up a
few bizarre tales myself at those dinner parties. I stepped out of
my life for a time, trying so hard to be what Benjamin saw in
me. A rough diamond, waiting to be polished by the blaze of his
brilliance, his love. The girls in the lecture halls have choices
now, and perhaps I did too, but it never occurred to me. Not
even when I left once, the first year we were married. After a
horrible fight, after a party where I'd sat silent, stupid, trying to
follow the darting, swooping conversation. Watching him
charm every woman in the room with his talk, his slender
hands. We shouted and cried and he struck me on the cheek,
not very hard, and I put on my coat and walked out of the
house and he threw a cup or a bottle, it crashed against the
door frame after I had gone through and he shouted, 'Good rid-
dance, who needs you — who needs you?'

I went back to the farm very calmly, deadly, and I cooked

and I cleaned and I drove in the cattle and I waited to see what would happen. He came for me a few days later. It was just before dawn, when the sky was grey and still, and he left the car on the road and walked up the lane and the low leaves of trees brushed his hair and the long wet grass soaked his feet, soaked his pant legs to the knee. He walked around to the back of the house; he hadn't shaved and his eyes were wild and he stood below my window and tipped his head back and he shouted 'Helen! Hel — en!' until his throat ached.

I was in the barn, collecting eggs. I came up behind him and took his hand.

When he was working on the Helen Poems we took the children to Greece for a year, rented a house on a small island. It didn't cost much but it still used up all our savings and when we came back I had to work for a while, typing essays and reports. 'If I could have stayed in Greece,' he often used to say, 'I would have been a great poet. That wonderful clear light, the inspiration of those ancient skies. Ah — if only I could have stayed, things would have been different.'

Well, perhaps, but I don't remember much clear light. The rented house squatted on a rocky hillside, no electricity or running water except for the rain that trickled through all winter. Michael was five and kept wandering away, Jennie trailing after him, and Alison was still in diapers and wouldn't let me out of her sight. Benjamin went for long walks and worked outside beneath a flowering fig tree, if the weather was fine.

The Helen Cycle was supposed to make his name, and some of it is quite lovely. The book was reviewed kindly, on the whole, and sections are still included in anthologies occasionally. 'Helen Weeping' was at one time used in a high school text. Benjamin grew a beard and got tenure and began to work on a second collection. It never appeared, although a few of the poems were printed here and there. There were times when, glass in hand, he would point to me and say, 'My Helen. Well, you see ...' And people in the room would begin to talk loudly about other things. And there were times when he would rage about the house, waving a fistful of bills and shouting that we were destroying him, bleeding him dry. We lived like that for years.

The first heart attack frightened him; he stopped smoking and drinking, began to walk to the campus and home, all about the town. He stood in front of the mirror in the bedroom, patting his flat stomach and saying, 'Look at that — I'm in better shape than when I was twenty. I feel better than I have in years.'

When they tried to reach me from the hospital I was in bed with Jonas, a quiet man who worked at the post office. We had been meeting on his lunch hour for several months; he had grown noticeably thinner, but never complained. I have thought since that at the moment that Benjamin's chest exploded I was probably stabbing my tongue at the base of my lover's spine. Some people would see that as a sign: crime and punishment. Benjamin would, for he is a very moral person; he believes in punishment. But I know that it was just a fluke of timing. I could just as easily have been vacuuming the spare room, pushing a cart through the supermarket. Which is where I said I was, to make things easier.

I've never told him about Jonas, about the others. In the old days, of course, there were his students. All those bright young boys who couldn't impress him any other way. Benjamin was always a good teacher but he loves a mocking phrase and was often, I am sure, quite cruel, carried away by the sound of the words.

So the young boys came to dinner, came to parties, came to seminar meetings held in our living room with a great deal of wine. And sometimes they would rise to help me, to carry dishes to the kitchen, pour coffee, open a bottle. And sometimes our fingers brushed, reaching for a coffee cup, an ashtray, and sometimes they called me, wrote letters, said there was no

one else in the world, and sometimes I thought — but only for a
moment. They were just boys, after all; they would have
wanted people to know, to guess. The men I have chosen have
been different, and they have had nothing to do with Benjamin's world. The carpenter who built our kitchen cupboards,
more than twenty years ago. The man who sold us insurance,
the high school chemistry teacher. Jonas, who I suppose was the
last. All kind, lonely men who wanted simply to give and
receive pleasure.

Benjamin has never known; he has never tried to know,
although I am sure the signs have been there. For years I wore a
silver locket, given to me by Phil, the insurance man.

And if he had known where I was when the hospital called,
he would have had to make it ridiculous. Geriatric desire — my
sagging thighs, the fringe of reddish hair around Jonas's skull.
Oh yes, I can just hear him. For years I tried to make him
happy, tried so hard to be what he thought I was. The silent
beauty in the stationery shop. 'Helen by the sea, with children'.
I never got it right, and sometime during the years of Scotch
and rage it ceased to matter. I looked at him across a crowded
room, heard him talk, his face flushed and a glass unsteady in
his hand, and I knew it didn't matter what I did, what I was. I
saw him then as a child, lost in the scent of pine needles. When
all the presents have been unwrapped with laughter and a
flurry of crackling paper and it slowly begins to be clear that
that one perfect, mysterious, longed-for gift is not there.

Later that evening he read a new poem, called 'Shanidar'.
And not long after, we had our kitchen remodelled.

*She's made her bed*, they used to say, where I come from. And I
have been close to saying it myself at times, listening to conver-
sations in restaurants and bus shelters. Or when my daughters
call from different parts of the world, talking about leaving a
husband or lover. How did you stand it? they say. All those
years with Daddy when he was — the way he used to treat you,

the way he used to carry on — why did you put up with all that?

I don't know, I tell them. I just did. I do.

And the wires hum with their anger and pain and then they say, What about the girls though, what about all those girls.

Ah yes, the girls. The girls who came to parties with all those gentle boys, the girls whose eyes sparkled in the light of tall candles. The girls whose names came up frequently, at home. A student of mine said ... wrote ... quite a clever girl really ... Angela. Or Christine, or Sarah. I always knew. I learned that each one would fade away, eventually, but they still caused me a great deal of pain. And maybe that's why I don't tell my daughters the rest of it, the funny part. How now that it doesn't matter I've come to think that he never slept with any of those girls. Something he said to me in the hospital, where I don't suppose a man would lie. All those grand, unconsummated, poet's loves.

The second attack enraged him. 'I might have known,' he said, in a voice thick with significance, 'that my heart would betray me after all.'

He has not accepted it easily. Retirement and a quiet life, the pacemaker which he blames now for the death of his poetry. He reviews books caustically and is lavishly hospitable to the occasional old student who comes by. He has set up a telescope in the back yard and memorized the known sky, tried to teach me to play chess. He follows his doctor's orders grudgingly, with small flashes of rebellion. A cigar at Christmas, a glass of brandy. I can see him now through the window, rake in his hand beneath a curdled autumn sky. He is not supposed to exert himself, but on a brisk October day, breathing deeply and wearing a navy watch cap to keep the heat in, he stirs the flame-coloured leaves very slowly.

And now that it no longer matters, there is something I would like to tell him. Something I have learned, about archaeology. When Heinrich Schliemann came at last to Hissarlik, he was sure that his lost city must lie in the deepest heart of the mound, and he gouged an enormous trench through the hill. But when he reached the deepest layer, none of it made sense. And he died without ever knowing that he had found his fabled Troy, much closer to the surface. That he had destroyed most of it, in his haste to reach the depths.

But then, as I watch through the window, I am suddenly ambushed by memory. A clear spring night in that rented house in Greece. Benjamin out walking and I had soothed the children to sleep, boiled water on the tiny gas burner, washed the dishes. And he burst through the door, his cheeks flaming and his eyes wide with magic. 'Come on, come with me,' he said, grabbing my hand.

And I went, surprised, a little grumpily, still holding the dishrag in my other hand. He pulled me into the night, stumbling down the rocky path to the point where the sea became visible. All bathed in silver, the whispering sea and the hillside behind us, the huddled white houses.

'Look at that moon,' he said, very softly. 'Oh Helen, just look at that moon.'

# Peach

I'm thinking about peaches, thinking about the way things get done. This is the day after a funeral. I'm thinking about my own fingers, sticky with juice, slicing peaches into a bowl and wondering if that was why the knife slipped, why I baked three drops of my blood into a pie. It has rained all night and the trees are dripping, sodden mounds of leaves in all the bruised shades of peaches cover the grass, the sidewalks and roads. There is music playing, viola; it circles around and around but never seems to arrive at the centre, the point.

I learn some facts about peaches by opening the old encyclopedia, releasing the smell of someone else's house on a rainy afternoon. I read that the peach probably came from China, like fireworks and pasta, that Spanish explorers brought it to the New World, that for centuries its cultivation was confined to the gardens of the nobility. On the same page I read that the African peacock (*afropavo congensis*) was discovered in 1936, after a search that began in 1913 with the finding of a single feather.

But about the peach, I read that it develops from a single ovary that ripens into a fleshy, juicy exterior and a hard interior called the stone or pit. I read that peach trees are intolerant of severe cold, but require some winter chilling to induce them to burst into growth after a dormant period. Also that most varieties produce more fruit than can be fully developed, that some shedding of fruitlets takes place naturally but the number remaining may have to be further reduced.

I'm thinking about peaches because I baked a peach pie on the day of Maisie's funeral. Thinking about peaches so I don't have to think about Maisie, who lived long enough to sit slumped in a chair in a hallway, long enough for everyone to think she'd already been dead for years. Thinking about the burnished skin of peaches, glistening with droplets of water in a blue bowl. Thinking about the texture of the flesh and the sudden stone at the heart, looking like something you would never expect. You would expect the smooth seeds of the orange, the delicate pips of apple or pear. But not the gnarled pit of the peach, full of rough, hidden places, so hard to work free.

And thinking about peaches takes me back to a hospital room, one I thought I'd done with years ago. Outside that long dark window autumn rain fell through the flickering street-lights, steady and cold. Inside, where we were, the radiator gurgled and your breathing machine hissed and thumped. *I'm here*, I whispered, but nothing changed. And I slid my palm beneath yours on the sheet, and my body remembered how it used to feel, reaching up to take your hand, and the way we walked with the sun going down over the lake, pine needles and sand soft beneath our feet. And of all the times we had done that, there seemed to be one particular time I yearned towards. I thought of a little house in a cave of trees, of the light glowing behind the windows, a door opening. As if it were the heart of some mystery, the centre of something I needed to understand, or at least remember.

In the hospital the sheet was rough, your hand a dry, frail thing, and I wondered where you had gone.

In those days there were still trains, and that was how she first came there. The train ran along the edge of the lake and the afternoon sun reflected so brightly that she had to close her eyes. And once her eyes were closed the rhythm of the train took over, and the rhythm of the train said *help-me help-me help-me*. She opened her eyes, astonished, and made herself look at the other passengers. An old man with luxuriant eyebrows, a woman in a pale dress with several young children, two older women with small brown hats. All people going home from somewhere, she was sure. Sure that she was the only one travelling to a completely new place.

She had come because of Maisie's letter mostly, but there were other reasons. Because she had struck a child, because her father had burned his tongue on the soup. She often thought of that, years later. Looking through a rain-streaked window, something bubbling on the stove behind her. Her father waited until she sat down, unfolded his heavy napkin, picked up the gleaming spoon and dipped it into the bowl with a little *chink*, grimaced and made a *tch* sound as it touched his lips, his tongue. That was all, but in that sound she heard everything. That it was all her fault, that she had made the soup, brought it to the table too hot, failed to warn him. That he would not complain, that he was tolerant and reasonable, that she did her best but it was not good enough.

That alone wouldn't have done it, of course, without Maisie's letter lying on her bedside table. Without the incident with the boy. No one would blame her for hitting him, and in theory she wouldn't have blamed herself. She'd been warned about him, a troublemaker from the start. A shifty-eyed child in mismatched clothes, always muttering and whistling under his breath, always picking at the sores around his mouth and nose. There was a strange flash of satisfaction in his pale eyes as her hand came down; she noted that with some cool part of her brain, but didn't remember it until later. For what really shook her, as her hand met flesh, was the thrill of white-hot fury, the way she could have gone on and on, the struggle to make herself stop. Sitting back at her desk with the boy snivelling in his seat, having the others stand and read, one by one, her nails digging into her palms until she could dismiss them and flee to the cloakroom. She was not a fool; she understood that her life was not as it seemed.

The train made its way along the lake to the tiny red brick station. Pausing on the dim step she saw the blaze of light that was the outside world, saw her own right foot in its laced shoe, the toe pointing down in the act of stepping out, already warmed by that light while the rest of her stayed in shadow. *This will be something*, she thought suddenly as her other foot met the ground, raising a small puff of yellow dust.

*Please come*, Maisie's letter had said. *There'll be all those old women telling me how to take care of a baby, but I'll need some real company.* So she knew about the baby but she was not prepared for how Maisie looked, her face rounder and dark hair curling around her cheeks in the heat, the way she seemed to be so full of life, bursting with it. They had known each other at the Education College, talked and laughed in Maisie's little room where she hoarded crumbs of food from her infrequent visits home. The boarding house was clean but cramped, the other boarders set in their ways. Still, Grace couldn't help envying the life as she hurried home through darkening streets, blowing her breath before her, her mind already preparing her father's dinner.

So they studied together and fretted together and walked giddily down rain-soaked streets. They thought they would be friends forever, but Grace stayed in the city and Maisie went back to teach in the country school near the place where she was born. Then she wrote to say she was marrying a boy she'd known all her life; their wedding trip brought them to the city for a day or two, but Grace and her father had gone for their annual visit to the cousins in Detroit. Maisie had to give up the school after the wedding, of course, but she was busy all day on the farm and she wrote letters about all the things she was pickling and preserving, in a way to make Grace laugh.

The young man standing beside Maisie in the summer sun had hair the colour of polished wood, and a soft blue shirt with the sleeves rolled up to the elbow.

'You must be Jim,' Grace said, holding out her hand, startled by Maisie's whoop of laughter as his fingers met hers.

'No no no,' Maisie said, 'Jim's haying. This is Harry. He

wants to show off his new car, so I said he could drive us out.'

Grace wondered later if she'd had some inkling in that first moment of the new way her life would go. Things seemed charged and strangely clear, but she thought that was just the daze of the journey, the bright sunlight falling all around them. They climbed into the car and drove through the town, which was gone before she had time to even notice it. A wide, dusty main street, a few drowsing horses hitched to wagons, a small boy pulling at a sitting dog on the end of a rope.

'My father had the first car in town,' Harry said. 'Before the war. But it was nothing like this beauty.'

She noticed how his voice drew out the word *beauty*. Then they were climbing the hill at the edge of town, sunlight slashing at the lake in the distance, and out in the open country where the sound of their travelling made conversation impossible. Harry's hands were square and easy on the steering wheel, although his eyes were narrow with concentration.

'I promised Jim I'd drive slow with Maisie along,' he shouted. 'But later I'll take you for a spin and show you what she can really do.'

Grace just smiled, holding her hair down with both hands.

Grace soon learned that Harry was a terrible tease, and she herself the kind of person who made it easy for him. That first day he told her all the things he'd found in the stomachs of fish caught in the lake. A diamond ring, a baby's rattle, a set of keys, a soggy prayer book. At the prayer book Grace realized she'd made a proper fool of herself, saying *Goodness*, and *How could that be*; she was grateful that he didn't seem to hold it against her. In the sunlight on the front porch he handed her a peach from a basket near his feet, and it seemed much more he was offering her.

Maisie's Jim, when he finally appeared, was a bit of a surprise. Looking so much like one of those fresh-faced country boys she had described, the ones she was so glad to be away from in the city. Red hair slicked down and all those freckles, even on the backs of his hands. He had hands that would look clumsy hanging down from a jacket sleeve, or holding a pen or a pencil. Resting briefly on top of Maisie's head as he passed by. He didn't talk much but you could tell how he felt about things, just by looking at him looking at Maisie.

Later that night, after Harry had gone and Jim had climbed the creaking back stairs, they sat up talking in the kitchen and it was just like the old days in the boarding house on Cobb Street. Except that Maisie was greedy for details and Grace could supply them. What women were wearing in the city, what shops had closed, what new places opened. She was like a person cramming for an examination, like someone galloping to the end of a good book, eager to start on the next. Grace wondered again why she hadn't stayed, why she had come back to the place she was so eager to get away from, but she couldn't ask. Not sitting in the solid farmhouse kitchen, not looking at Maisie's thickened fingers, resting on her huge belly. Once, pushing herself up from the chair, she paused, her knuckles white on the table, and said, 'Oh Grace, how'd I get myself into this.' But then she laughed and Grace thought she'd been joking. She'd already seen the chest of baby clothes, each stitch tiny and immaculate, although Maisie claimed to be useless at such things.

It was very hot those first two weeks, the countryside shimmering, filled with the sound of clicking insects. Harry came several times to take Grace driving, along dusty twisting roads, over rackety bridges where they could look down and see small boys wading in the sluggish river. Sometimes they stopped at a little store or a farmhouse and drank something cold before going on, and Grace told him things that surprised her, things that were true, and yet not true. Like about Arthur being killed in France — it was true that she wrote him every week, true that she packed up tin boxes filled with jam and candy and warm woollen socks. It was not true that he'd meant any more to her than all the other boys she went to school with, but that was the part she didn't say. True that she helped her father with his research, although usually that just meant transcribing his scribbled notes. With Harry she felt like someone who fit the facts of her life, someone she could, perhaps, become.

Going around with Harry she learned that he knew everyone, not just by name but by history. As they drove away he would tell her strange, scandalous things about the old man who'd poured them a glass of lemonade, the woman waving from the farmyard gate.

'That can't be true,' Grace would say, laughing and holding her hair.

'I swear,' Harry said, turning his head to look her straight in the eye.

There were moments like that, when Harry looked right at her, that everything else disappeared. But she told herself that was nonsense, that he only took her about because Maisie asked him to. One night, after Harry had been to supper, Maisie said he should take Grace to the party he was going on to. A little house in the little town where everyone knew him and slapped him on the back, knew who Grace was too and smiled at her. The house was overflowing, rugs rolled back and people stomping on the floor in time to the fiddles played by three old men sitting on kitchen chairs. They sat on the grass just outside, Harry resting on his elbows with his legs stretched out in front, feet crossed at the ankles and moving in time to the music. Grace thought she had never seen someone so completely at home in the world. On the tail of that thought, Harry spoke out of the dark.

'Do you ever think,' he said, 'that things are just too easy?'

'No,' Grace said, 'no, I never have found that.'

It was very late when Harry drove her home, the car like a cocoon moving through the dark countryside and she thought that he might kiss her then, and he did.

Maisie was waiting up in the darkened kitchen; she had trouble sleeping these last days. Grace didn't see her at first, just heard her voice coming harshly out of the dark.

'Well, you have the look of a girl in love,' Maisie said, but Grace just laughed.

They sat up talking, as they usually did, and most of their talk was about Harry. He didn't say much about himself, but Maisie seemed to know every detail and Grace thought it strange, since she knew him so well, that she had never talked about him in the city. That night Maisie told her about Harry's mother, how she'd walked into the river behind their house, leaving him a baby sleeping in a buggy. His father found him there, out on the riverbank, when he came home for lunch. It was the talk of the town, of course, but no one could find an explanation. All the books, perhaps. And then the way his father married again, but a child does need a mother, after all.

And Grace almost wept, sitting there at the kitchen table; she could see it all so vividly. The baby that was Harry, cooing and waving his arms about. The woman in something long and white walking smoothly backwards, her eyes on her child until the last possible moment. It gave Harry an added dimension, this story, as if he carried within himself the dappled riverbank, the sound of willow leaves in the wind, the rushing water. She thought this even after she saw a photograph of Harry's mother, hanging on the wall. Large and heavy-featured, she looked like a woman just waiting to roll up her sleeves and get on with something. A women who, having made up her mind, would stride into the cold water without a backward glance.

Maisie wanted them all to have a picnic at the lake, but it was too close to her time to go driving so far in a car or wagon. So they set up a table outside the house, packed everything in a big hamper and unloaded it on a flowered cloth. The table was under an ash tree, bright red berries clustering, and Maisie sat on a kitchen chair with her back to the house so she could pretend it was a real picnic.

'It *is* a real picnic,' Harry said, and to prove it he produced two bottles of last year's cider and they all drank it and got quite giddy. Jim started to laugh at something Harry had said; he laughed with a helpless, whooping giggle that got them all going, holding on to their aching sides. Grace thought of the rain-coloured rooms of her father's house, thought, *This is where I belong, right here with these wonderful people.*

Jim went to check something in the barn and the three of them stayed around the table, talking. A fellow Maisie and Harry knew who was in the veterans' hospital, how his wife still took the train to see him every week, five years later. Grace knew that Harry had just missed the war, had been on his way, in England, when the bells rang. He hadn't said, but she supposed he would feel guilty about that; relieved, and guilty about that too. Maisie told them about her plan to have Grace stay. She said the young fellow who'd taken over her school wasn't working out, that she was sure the trustees would hire Grace in a minute. They could find her a little house in town, she knew just the place.

'Harry'd like that, wouldn't you, Harry,' she said, and her voice was loud although she was smiling like always.

For some reason not clear to any of them, Maisie decided she wanted to taste a red berry. She climbed onto her chair, then onto the table, planting her feet apart on the flowered cloth, reaching up. *That's dangerous,* Grace thought, but lazily, for Maisie was laughing as she picked a cluster of berries, laughing and saying, 'What do I do now? How do I get down from here?' And Harry was laughing too; he got to his feet, opened his arms wide and said, 'Jump — I'll catch you.'

There was a moment when she could have stopped herself; Grace, watching, saw that moment come and go. Then a long, slow moment when her huge shape hung in the air, before it collided with Harry, before they both went crashing to the ground. Maisie came up still laughing, pushing herself until she was half sitting, and cuffed him hard across the head, saying 'Aren't I the great ninny then, thinking you really could.'

The next night the baby was born dead, and Harry asked Grace to marry him. She thought about that later, how it hadn't seemed strange at all. Thought about poor Jim with his freckled hands hanging heavy and useless and Maisie pale and weak in the upstairs bedroom, her eyes flat and the terrible sobbing that went on and on until finally she slept.

Harry was sitting on the porch steps, smoking a cigarette and looking into the night. She sat down beside him and he put his arm around her; she rested her head on his shoulder, too tired to care what he thought. The lights from the house fell golden on the grass in front of them, beyond that only the mysterious shaped of trees, brooding and rustling a little.

'Would you ever think of marrying a fool like me,' Harry said, and she said, 'I would. Yes I would.'

Harry was a joker and a tease and his wit was often cutting. Cut Grace. When she first knew him he forgave her for that, but later he became impatient. 'Oh, I was only joking,' he'd say. 'Can't you take a joke, Grace?' And then he'd get angry and the lightness would be spoiled and it would be all her fault. He taught their children that, that she couldn't take a joke, and she knew that no matter how many times they'd seen her laugh, that would be part of the picture they had of her. Part of the role she played, like hosting teas and baking things for sales and carefully choosing a new hat for church. She was astonished to realize, in her later years, that this was her life. She'd thought it was something she was moving towards, the same way she'd thought she was moving towards Harry. Thought she would some day come to understand the contradiction that he was, all that teasing and then his black days, days when he wouldn't speak a word, when he'd sit in a darkened room or sometimes in the car in the driveway and not answer whoever came to call him for supper.

He came back after his black days, he always did, and she allowed it. She thought perhaps that was why he had chosen her, why he had seemed so sure. That he recognized some darkness in her, or some respect for darkness that would permit things that someone like Maisie would only snort at in her gruff and sunny way.

In the beginning they saw a lot of each other, the four of them having meals together or an evening of cards, going to the fall fair. Then in the fifth year of their marriage Jim fell from a high place in the barn, and everyone wondered what he'd been doing up there. Maisie though he'd been after a kitten that had got itself stuck. 'He's such a softie,' she said, 'that would be just like him.'

Jim had probably been dead for hours when Maisie found him, had gone looking when he didn't come in for dinner. The kitten, if there had been a kitten, was long gone.

At the funeral Maisie was very calm, although hours before she'd been howling in Grace's arms in the cold kitchen. Raving about how Jim didn't deserve it, how she was a terrible woman. Grace reminded her how much Jim had loved her, how plain it was to see, but that didn't help and in the end she could only smooth her hair until the terrible crying stopped. She supposed it was something to do with the baby; she knew they'd had some trouble over that. Jim wanting them to have more, and Maisie holding back.

Jim's brothers took over the farm, as was only fair. Maisie walked away leaving almost everything behind — the big double bed, the pictures on the wall, curtains in the windows. They paid her enough money to buy a house in town, the same little house she'd thought of for Grace that first summer. People talked about the bare windows but Maisie just shrugged her shoulders and said, 'I've got no secrets to hide.' Said, 'If they don't like what they see, they shouldn't be looking in.'

Grace knew her stubbornness and so while her own babies were sleeping she stitched and stitched until she'd made brightly coloured curtains for every room of the little house. One wild fall day she piled them into the buggy and wheeled them over, the blue air filled with spiralling coloured leaves. The house was set back from the road and looked quite nice; Harry had been helping to paint and hammer things into place. It was planted with pine trees all around, not maples and elms like the farm, but they were still quite small and Grace felt like a giant, striding to an enchanted cottage. They hung the curtains and then drank tea, cupping their hands to warm them in the little kitchen with its table and two chairs. Until the children started to grizzle and she took them home, pausing to look back and feeling quite pleased at the way everything was decently covered and Maisie waving cheerfully from the front door.

Harry's father was dead and his stepmother had moved away and he lived still in the square stone house and that was where he brought Grace, after they were married. He didn't mind what she did, so she set about changing every room, painting and papering and buying furniture. Their four children were born, one right after the other, and she found that whole months could pass without her having what she would have called a serious thought. She was blissfully happy.

It was during that time that Maisie fell apart, for a while. Telephoning late at night, in a state, and Harry would put on his trousers and go to her. Well of course Grace couldn't walk through the sleeping town, leaving her little ones.

'She was *drunk*,' he said, the first time he came back.

Maisie had taken a job in the school just outside of town, walking the two miles there and back in all kinds of weather. Often she was late, the children racing inside to sit at their desks when they saw her appear on the crest of the last hill.

Through the windows they watched her stop at the pump in the yard and duck her whole head under. There was talk, but people made allowances.

Grace's father had been heavily sarcastic about the life she was going to. He referred to Harry as 'your young farmer' although he knew very well that he was a lawyer, like his own father, and an educated man. He feigned astonishment when she told him they would live in a large stone house, not a cabin made from rough-hewn logs. Grace told herself that he was just covering the fact that he would miss her, but she had an uneasy suspicion that he might, in fact, be exactly what he seemed, a terrible snob.

He came to stay with them each Christmas, complaining about the journey and about the draughts in the house, although Grace knew well that it was warmer than his own. She thought that he might soften, holding his grandchildren on his knee, but he took little notice of them unless they behaved badly and he could criticize their upbringing.

During the rest of the year she telephoned every Sunday evening, until once he didn't answer and she knew that it was exactly as she imagined — his cold body lying somewhere in the big dark house while the telephone rang and rang. She called the neighbours, paced her downstairs rooms until they called back, their voices tight with the drama of it all. She was surprised that she didn't grieve more, all those years they'd spent together. She did find, though, that she thought more about her mother than she had in years. Grace was eight when she died and when she thought of that time, she remembered her mother paddling away in a canoe, over a calm lake with the sun going down. This was not likely ever to have happened; her mother was not athletic, and where would they have kept a canoe? Still, the image was so clear that she had always accepted it as part of her string of memories. It was only when she thought about it that it became strange, like someone else's memory, or a dream.

She didn't tell her children about that, when they came to an age of wanting stories of her life. There was little enough to interest them, she thought, and so she told them stories from Maisie's life instead. 'Tell us,' they would say, with the covers pulled up to their chins, 'tell us about the time there was a blizzard and Maisie had to sleep in the school all night. And they ran out of wood and had to burn all their notebooks so they didn't freeze into ice blocks. Tell us the time the goose chased Maisie away from the outhouse, the time she drove the big wagon and the horses ran away. Tell us the time Maisie put stuff on her hair and it turned bright orange and she had to wear a scarf for weeks. Tell us a Maisie story.'

After a few months Maisie wasn't late for school any more, although there were still days when she slept with her head on the desk while the older children helped the younger ones with their sums, or listened to them read aloud. She stopped calling in the night, which was just as well because Harry was out most evenings at some meeting or other, coming home late, tired and not talking. But she also stopped dropping by; they hardly ever saw each other and when she had time to think of it, Grace missed the giddy days of their friendship. She invited Maisie to teas, to Sunday dinner, an evening of bridge, but she usually cried off at the last minute. A headache, a toothache, a pile of examinations to mark.

Grace thought it was probably her fault, thought she'd grown boring, surrounded by her babies. Some days she thought it was hard for Maisie, seeing her with her family, and some days she thought the fading away was just part of growing up, of having a mature life. It was ridiculous, really, how long it took her to work it out. Her youngest child was starting high school; they were coming out of church one blue Sunday morning, Grace caught a little behind. Maisie stumbled on the bottom step, and in the way Harry reached out to steady her, Grace suddenly saw it all. In the unthinking, automatic way he took her arm, then let it go, without even having to look at her, to say a word. It hit Grace like a fist to the stomach, and she felt such a fool.

That particular Sunday they had invited Maisie for lunch; Grace took to her bed and heard them all downstairs, laughing and talking. Maisie tiptoed upstairs later to see how she was feeling and the bed creaked when she sat on it. Grace's jaw clenched so tight she could barely hiss, 'Get out of here.'

'I thought you knew,' Maisie said that night on the telephone. 'Oh Grace, I thought you always knew.'

She set the telephone down, hard.

Grace stayed in her bed for a week with a terrible, aching fatigue, rearranging everything she knew about her life. Her youngest daughter carried bowls of soup up the stairs, smoothed her hair from her forehead, and she wept to think someone would be so kind to her. Harry sat on the side of the bed, holding her hand and saying it was all over, saying he was sorry, and she turned her face away. She felt such a fool for all the years of trying to learn Harry, for feeling they could arrive at some place together when she'd been hobbled all along, without even knowing. Everything was shaky now, and she wondered about those days long ago. She remembered that hot summer, Harry holding out a peach and what happened with their eyes when she met his gaze; now she wished she could push the frame out and see the look on Maisie's face. She thought about that first day, the puff of yellow dust rising around her leather shoe and she thought she could get on a train again, ride it into another new life, but she knew she wouldn't. She thought about those nights sitting up in the kitchen, Maisie's hands clasped on her swollen belly, talking about Harry, and she groaned and turned her face into the pillow.

But what do you do when your heart is breaking? In the end, you just go on. Grace rose from her bed after a week with a feeling that something had hardened inside her, something that would never be soft again. She thought she wouldn't speak to Maisie for the rest of her life, but of course that's not how it worked out. The town was small; they were always running into each other in the butcher's, the drugstore, on a sunny corner. The part of Grace that cared had turned to stone and she found that it wasn't so hard to say a few words and then walk on. Not even hard to face Harry across the supper table, to watch his hair turn gray. To go with him on winter trips to Florida, to stroll on the beach with her arm in his, to watch their children marry, one by one. Years went by, ten years, twenty, and it was only sometimes that she thought of the smooth sheen of a peach in Harry's brown hand, and knew that it could have been another way.

When Annie's baby died they brought their other granddaughter to stay for the summer and Grace thought how good it was, to have a child living in the house again. One night she made a special supper of all the girl's favourite things; Harry was having one of his days and didn't eat with them. The child sat at the table with a colouring book while Grace washed the dishes and when she was wringing out the cloth she caught sight of herself in the curved side of the big corn pot. Without thinking any more about it she called the child to come for a walk and they moved through the long shadows of the town, through summer air scented with flowers, until they came to the place where light glowed behind Maisie's windows in the little house set back from the road. They walked through a grove of evergreens, grown so tall, and knocked on the blue front door. And Maisie opened it, as if she'd always known she would.

I'm thinking about peaches the day after a funeral, thinking about my grandmother and the way we used to walk when the sun was going down. Thinking about my grandfather in the dark house behind us, and how we left without a word. How once we came to a house in a cave of trees, all the night birds settling there. 'My friend Maisie lives here,' my grandmother said, and I remembered all those stories my mother liked to tell, and missed her with a sudden pain.

The woman who opened the door was wearing an old plaid dressing gown and her face was scrubbed and shining. 'Oh Grace,' was all she said. Inside she turned on more lights and the night leapt black beyond the windows. They sat me on a couch with a game of jacks that came from a little string bag, while they sat at the kitchen table, their hands wrapped around mugs of tea. They talked and talked but I didn't understand a word they said.

After a long time they started to laugh and then they called me into the kitchen. 'You must try these peaches I've got,' Maisie said. 'They taste like a mouthful of summer.' She turned from the sink as she spoke and light flashed from the blade of the dripping knife, from her shiny forehead and cheeks. My grandmother was wiping her eyes; she said she was happy, not sad.

Maisie reached for a plate and the knife flashed again. She set it down in front of me, resting a cool, wet hand on my head and saying, 'There you go, sweetheart,' as if she'd never known my name. Their voices swooped and laughed over me as I stared at the thing on the thick green plate. A peach split in half with an aching hole in the centre, wriggling red lines pulsing out from that place. I was sure I would taste blood, and I did when I bit into it and something thickened in my throat and my eyes were suddenly running with tears. My grandmother took me in her lap, as if I were much smaller, and rocked me back and forth and when the tears finally stopped I felt lighter than air. At the door Maisie pressed something into my hand, something hard and rough. 'Take this,' she said. 'And if you plant it well, maybe something will grow.'

# Down by the Lake

Down by the lake Jess says, 'I've been thinking about that yellow mixing bowl,' and Babe says, 'Uh huh.' Then she waits while Jess gives her purse a shake, listening for the chink of the car keys. Jess does this every so often as they walk but it's not because she's old. Her whole life she's had the feeling she could easily misplace something important.

'Just look at that,' she says, and Babe knows she's talking about the sight of her bare foot on the hard sand. Its paleness and the thickened nails and the cords and bumps all over the place. It looks an alien thing, although the sad truth is that it fits right in with the way the rest of their bodies look now, getting ready for bed at night.

'Remember Miss Earnshaw?' Babe says, and Jess says, 'Uh huh.' On a Sunday school excursion to Kincardine once. Miss Earnshaw grew up in China, became a missionary like her parents. Her face was very wrinkled and a strange, yellowish shade — from living there so long, everyone supposed. On the beach she sat down on a flat rock and took off her shoes and stockings to shake the sand out. She was missing two toes on her right foot.

On the way home the motion of the train sent them all to sleep and when Babe opened her eyes Miss Earnshaw was shaking her shoulder, her yellow face so close Babe could see something wet and glistening in the deep folds that ran down from the corners of her mouth. She screamed; she couldn't help it. After that they scared each other at night, going up the long dark stairs. Hauling on the banister and thumping their feet unevenly, each pretending to be Miss Earnshaw, coming to get the other.

\* \* \*

Although it's still August the air is getting cooler down by the lake as the sun begins to fade. It's one of those evenings when the water is flat and still, a soft greenish-grey like a dress Babe had once, and sound carries a long way. They can hear people setting tables in the cottages they walk by, and mothers telling children to wash their hands right now. At one place they pass a girl turning cartwheels in a circle on the cool sand; she doesn't even look at them.

'How old was Catherine?' Jess says, although she knows very well. 'Nine,' Babe says, knowing that Jess knows, that the question is just a way to start them thinking. They've lived together so long that it only needs a word or phrase, sometimes even a look; they don't actually talk much, but their shared thoughts are a conversation that goes on all the time.

This year there's a tree trunk that's washed up from somewhere, lying across the beach just past the last cottage. Not a trunk, a whole tree really, but it's been worn so silvery smooth that it's all of a piece, the web of branches and the tufted base where the fine roots would have been. The way it lies it's just the right height and they lower themselves carefully. Jess reaches into her bag, jingling the keys, and brings out the battered cigarette case that belonged to their brother Roy. It was sent back from France with the rest of his things and for a long time it sat on a table in the front room with his badges and the picture he'd sent them, looking serious in his uniform and cap. Their mother was death on smoking and drinking, all that kind of thing. *Where would he get something like that*, she kept saying after she'd opened the package. They all knew it was from Adele, but didn't say a word. All five of them watching as he packed things up the night before he left. *Now don't tell Mother*, Roy said, showing them; *you know how she is.* And they all promised and none of them ever did tell.

Roy tucked the shiny cigarette case in with his thick socks

and his shadow was huge as he walked back and forth in the lamplight and he had to duck every time he came near the point where the roof sloped, over the head of his bed. Willie and Tom and Art dragged the heavy bag downstairs, stumbling over each other, and Roy came staggering after, carrying Jess and Babe on each arm as they liked him to do, even though they were far too heavy. Their arms touched around his neck.

'I wonder what they said to each other,' Jess says, thinking about their father with the wagon hitched up, white mist pluming from the horses' nostrils, waiting to drive Roy to meet the late train. Their father thought he was a fool to go when he was needed on the farm and when they got the news he said, *Dammit, I told him*, over and over and their mother didn't say a word though she was death on swearing too.

When the cigarette case came back it was scratched and chipped and dented and they thought that was from bullets and battles. For a while they thought it their duty to somehow give it back to Adele, but then their mother came back from town one day and said she'd actually seen her laughing, walking down the street, so they knew she didn't deserve it. It must have gone to one of the boys later, and then somehow made its way back to Babe and Jess. They are the last ones left and a lot of things have come back to them in cardboard boxes or old suitcases.

The tree trunk is already cooling in the evening air; they can feel it a little through the faded plaid wool trousers they wear. They sit puffing on their cigarettes, looking out through the clouds of tiny black flying things that hover near the water's edge. Farther down a boat roars out from the shore, cutting a path that takes a long time to heal.

'Poor Mother,' Jess says.

It wasn't fair, the way it took her near the end. The way she'd take off all her clothes and start to wander off downtown if you weren't watching her every minute. Some days there was nothing to be done but tie her in a chair. They never knew much about her early life or they might have been able to make some sense of the things she said. Calling out names that were not familiar to them, calling someone to bring a bucket, to catch that damn dog, to hush now, hush now. Sometimes she patted her knee, gingerly, as if she'd fallen down and scraped it. And sometimes she'd croon Jenny Jenny Jenny, over and over again. That was her own name.

They were already living in town then, in the old house Willie bought cheap after Mr Warren hanged himself. Willie kept saying he was going to get married and fill it with children, but he never did. None of them had children, unless maybe Art did and no one thought to tell them. He went out west on a harvest excursion, and never came back. Sent them a card when he got married, and once in a while after. Then a letter from his wife to say he'd died in an accident. She'd signed her full name, as if just *Eleanor* was too informal.

Certainly Tom never had any children, living out on the farm, getting stranger and stranger. Selling off the front field for those Boyds to fill up with wrecked cars.

'What a blessing Father didn't live to see that,' Jess says.

For a while Tom was a bootlegger; Babe heard talk when she taught in the high school. A big belly and an old undershirt, tufts of grey hair growing down the back of his neck. And that was the same Tom whose eyes glowed in the lamplight in Roy's room, who came running through the door yelling about Catherine falling, about the blood.

'Poor Mother,' Jess says again, and Babe says, 'Uh huh.'

'I don't remember any hugs or kisses, any dears or darlings,' Jess says, 'do you?'

She asks because Babe is almost two years older, because she's never quite sure she didn't miss out on something, forget something.

'No,' says Babe. 'But that wasn't her way, was it? She was

good to us though, never hit us, like some.'

'Just the once,' Jess says, and Babe says, 'Uh huh.'

On their way out of town to the lake they have to pass by the old farm, the place where it used to be.

'We could have been sitting pretty,' Babe always says, looking over; Jess keeps her eyes on the road and the red needle on the speedometer. When Tom died they found out that the bank owned the farm; they never have figured out what he did with the money. The last people that bought it tore down the old house, the barn, and made Amber Acres. Lot after lot, house after house, stretching all the way back to the bluff overlooking the lake.

In the old days it was all bush back behind, but there was a rough sort of road or path. You came through it and suddenly, what you never expected. The cry of gulls and crashing waves and water stretching as far as you could see. Babe said it was Michigan on the other side, far — even farther than the horizon. She knew things like that, when they were children. Babe went to high school, and then on to the Normal. She taught in a country school first, where the big boys who came in the winter chewed up wads of paper and flicked them off their rulers, all over the room. Then she taught geography in the high school for so long that her classes were filled with children of the children she'd taught.

They'd always said Jess had a weak heart, something that made the new young doctor laugh when she went to see him. *Sound as a bell*, he said. *You'll outlive me* — although she could tell by his curly sideburns, his moustache and bright green shirt, that he didn't really think that. But sound as a bell anyway, so she could have gone to high school after all, and then on to who knew what. A five-mile walk it was, there and back, and the first two days she was so tired she fell asleep at the supper table, fell right off her chair. But she was desperate to go, to keep going, and when they said it was too far, too hard with her weak heart, she begged her father to drive her in, but he refused. *Plenty to do right here,* he said, and her mother agreed. It was a shame, she was smart as a whip, everybody said. She read everything she could get hold of, and Babe shared everything she could, but it wasn't the same, she knew that. It was something she always felt the lack of, in company, in conversation. Something she got used to.

'Maybe they were just scared of losing you too,' Babe says, and Jess shrugs her shoulders a little.

'Those mornings I had to get up in the dark,' Babe says. 'Or when I boarded with that old couple out near Brussels.'

'The place with the corn husk tick?' Jess says, and Babe says, 'Uh huh. Don't believe I slept a wink that whole year. Lie there in the middle of the night with those lumps and bumps poking into me, thinking about that feather tick we had at home. And then thinking about all of you there in the house, sleeping and dreaming in the dark. Made me cry and cry and I was that envious of you, Jess, not having to go out in the world like me.'

'Uh huh,' Jess says; she's heard it before.

The sun is moving now and the sky is starting to take on colour — orange and mauve, a rich, pale blue. They push themselves up from the log, holding on to each other for a moment until they get their balance, and start to walk back to where they've parked the car, shoes sitting neatly on the front seat with the socks tucked inside.

'Those mornings he used to take you to meet the early train,' Jess says, 'when you were at the Normal. What did you talk about?'

They have reached a small, stony patch and pick their way carefully before Babe answers.

'I don't know at all,' she says. 'I can't remember a thing, do you know, I can't remember a thing he might ever have said.'

There was a story about Catherine as a baby; he must have

told that. One night she wouldn't settle and their mother was exhausted, at her wit's end. He carried Catherine downstairs in his stocking feet, stoked up the fire and sat holding her, watching it. And she quieted, watching the flames, and after a while she fell asleep on his chest and he sat there while the fire died, his nose so cold and his breath starting to show, afraid to move a muscle lest he wake her.

Catherine and Roy were the oldest and even though there wasn't much more than a year between any of them, it seemed like it must have been different. Like they were born to two different people, born out of something that couldn't help but be soon used up. Otherwise it was impossible to imagine.

The lake stretches away, vast beside them, and it's easy to understand how some first white man would have thought he'd reached the ocean. The bafflement when he found the water fresh.

'Well, you can only make the world from what you know,' Babe says. 'Build it up piece by piece from the things you believe to be true.'

After their mother died things were getting more expensive and they let out a room, the one at the top of the back stairs. The first time to the teacher who'd taken Babe's place at the high school, but it didn't work out. Strange noises and creaking stairs and one night Jess met the Durant boy putting on his shoes in the moonlit kitchen. After the teacher there was a clerk from the bank who blinked very fast when anyone spoke to him. He was quiet enough but one night he set the bedclothes on fire, didn't even wake up until Babe dumped a bucket of water over everything. Then Margaret Hatch from the grocery, who was no trouble at all.

Now they keep the upstairs closed off, to save on the heat and the stairs. They go up in the spring to dust and sweep, but that's about all. In the top drawer of a dresser up there is an old envelope, full of hair. Seven chunks of hair, each one tied with a bit of white ribbon, looking much the same. As if it didn't matter who they belonged to, but Jess wonders suddenly if her mother always knew. If she didn't need to distinguish because she just knew. She doesn't like it but she can't help thinking sometimes that maybe there's another side to everything she knows. That maybe hardness is sorrow. That a stony silence enfolds all the tenderness in the world.

It's getting dark as they drive slowly down the highway. They can't see the lake from where they are, but the coloured sky marks it for them. When they pass Amber Acres Babe doesn't say anything about the view. Instead what she says is, 'Will you still go down there?'

'Oh, I don't know,' Jess says. 'Maybe not.'

So far they've all died in order, sisters and brothers, and if what they told Babe at the medical centre is true, they still will. As they round the bend and start down the hill the lights of the town are all spread out below them and it looks quite grand and full of promise.

'Home again home again,' Jess says, like always, and Babe says, 'Uh huh.'

And then she says, 'We were just young, we didn't know any better.'

'That's so,' Jess says.

It doesn't seem possible that it was the same day, but that's how they remember it. Bitter cold and everything covered with ice, the branches of trees through the window like something out of a storybook, diamonds and daggers. The sharp-edged frozen ruts of the laneway. Their mother in her bluish apron standing, stirring. Babe and Jess on chairs, their chins resting on the kitchen table, staring at the yellow mixing bowl; she is making a cake and she has promised them that if they wait very still and quiet, they can lick out the bowl. Willie watching out the window, the big black winter window, watching for the older ones coming up the laneway, home from school. And then suddenly the yelling, Tom shrieking about blood, about Catherine falling, and Roy staggering, trying to carry her, their father running to meet them, slipping and sliding. Catherine's white, frozen face on the kitchen floor and all that blood from her head.

For some reason Babe and Jess are alone in the kitchen and they dip a finger into the batter in the yellow bowl and once they start they can't stop, it's the best thing they've ever tasted and then they're scooping it up in their small hands and it's running everywhere, between their fingers, over their chins. And their mother comes through a door and she says something or maybe nothing at all, and she grabs the wooden spoon from the bowl, batter flies everywhere, on the cupboard, on the wall, and she hits and hits and hits them, until the wooden spoon breaks in two.

# 1917

In those days it was very cold and we had to wear most of our clothes at the same time, in layers, and even that was not enough. And our breath looked different when it plumed ahead of us at night, though why that should be we had no idea. Why it should look different from our breath on a snowy night street back home, as if the very air had altered. Perhaps just what we had come from, what we were going to. For breath is breath, isn't it, and the most important thing of all.

In those days we rode trains all over the country and they were always cold and crowded, except when they were hot and crowded. The trains were filled with signs: *Taisez-vous, méfiez-vous, les oreilles ennemies vous écoutent.* For there were supposed to be spies everywhere in those days. Often, in Paris, if we were sitting in a restaurant with someone in uniform there would be a dapper man at the next table trying not to look like he was listening. It made us feel very strange to know someone had so much interest in our conversation. The same with the censor and that was one reason our letters home were always cheerful; the censor would return the ones with too much truth in them. But about the trains, in those days they were always late and they always stood still in the middle of nowhere for an hour, or two or three. So we were always hungry on trains, even if we'd brought something with us, even if we'd managed to buy a little pink ticket that would get us in for breakfast or lunch. Or sometimes a packet or two of cigarettes would do if we didn't have a ticket. In those days most of us learned to smoke and there was always some prissy fellow waiting to be shocked, to say we weren't that kind of woman, were we? As if you could know anything at all about a woman from that.

In those days we were all part of the machine. It started when we stepped on the boat, waved goodbye to our family and friends, although we didn't realize it right away. But maybe the first night when the steward screwed the porthole closed, pulled the heavy curtain, when we tried to sleep, heads on our bulky life preservers, in a small, stuffy cabin filled with the breath of strangers. If we'd thought about it at first we would have assumed that someone was guiding the machine, a room full of men somewhere, calm and in control. But the longer we were at the war the more clearly we saw that the machine ran itself, lurching around, creating its own momentum, spitting out mangled bodies as it went.

In those days some of us were nurses and we saw those bodies every day. Boys with no arms, no legs, no faces. And even if we had seen things before, factory accidents maybe, or falls from high places, we were unprepared. We changed dressings, touched hands, wrote letters which would be opened by a woman in a sunny room. And often there was a boy who was not expected to live and we put green screens around his bed and sometimes we sat with him for a little while, holding his hand while he struggled for breath. And the noises of the ward were all around us, the squeaking wheel of a cart, the rasp of a match, the voices of the others talking and joking, or moaning, and we thought how there was no privacy in a war, not even in death.

In those days we wrote long letters home and waited and waited for word to come back from a world that was increasingly remote. We had promised to write every day but usually we saved things up and tried to explain a week, or two, forgetting things that had seemed so important to pass on. Often we wrote in bed with our clothes on and all the covers pulled up because in those days it was very cold. Some of us had little stoves in our rooms and we walked home with our bundles of wood to burn, just like everyone else. We had brought hot water bags with us but they didn't help much although in the mornings we could empty the water out for a wash. We wrote these things to our mothers, making it sound like an adventure, for our mothers worried about us being cold and not clean. We tried to explain how it was on Saturdays when there was hot water, and how we'd never realized that a tub of hot water could seem like the most important thing in the world. We were careful to sound cheerful, not wanting to raise eyebrows at the breakfast table, to send someone racing to the telegraph office to summon us back.

In those days it *was* all a great adventure, until the first death. Maybe the boy with the shy smile, who was so polite, or the one who made us laugh out loud in the middle of a restaurant. Maybe the news came from home, a letter written from that shady street about someone we'd walked to school with every day. We wept in the dark in our cold rooms and after that it was still an adventure, but a real one.

In those days some of us were telephone operators and some of us could speak French and were in great demand and we all complained about the French operators, who said *Moment* and then went away forever. Everything was urgent in those days and some of us were right up near the front lines with our tin hats and gas masks hanging on a nail and the big guns pounding and sometimes the hut shook, sometimes we had to move out right away and if it hadn't been such a rush we would have been very afraid.

In those days most of us cut our hair, but unlike Samson it only made us stronger. Some of us learned to drive and sometimes we wore trousers and crawled under cars with a heavy spanner, humming *Madelon* and looking for something to fix.

In those days some of us were like Nancy and missed music most of all and we found a small piano in the back of a shop selling remnants of normal lives, and paid three boys not yet called up to hoist it four flights in the *pension*. And we started off playing Chopin but before long it was 'Pack Up Your Troubles' and 'Fancy You Fancying Me' and we all sang along until the cross woman below pounded on her ceiling with a broom or a stick and we had to stop.

In those days some of us lived in cheap hotels and some in camps and some of us took rooms with someone like Mme Charpentier, who owned two floors in a building on the Rue des Lilas. Mme Charpentier was tall with a long, thin nose; she had lost three sons and waited each day for word from two more. Their pictures were all lined up on the mantelpiece and sometimes her lip trembled in the ticking of the clock and she touched the frames with the tip of one finger. Also living there were three elderly cousins from the country, whose eyes grew moist when they talked of their beautiful *chateau*, now turned into a hospital with the grounds grown wild. The cousins sat in the *salon* all day, playing cards and reading the newspapers, wiping the smudges from their fingers with handkerchiefs they kept tucked in their sleeves. Mme Charpentier always apologized for the quality of the food when we sat down to dine with the silver gleaming even though there was only Lizette to polish it now.

In those days some of us worked in canteens in the camps, pouring coffee and hot chocolate from big pitchers, selling soap and cigarettes. We all looked like someone's mother, sister, girlfriend, and there was always someone wanting to talk to us because of that. Sometimes they talked of things they'd seen, blackened villages, rats, the pieces of a friend's body.

Sometimes things they liked to do back home. Climbing the tallest tree on a dare, playing piano at parties, stealing candy when they were young, how that felt. Sometimes dreams of the future. Now don't laugh, they always said as they started. And they always said how easy it was to talk to us, how they could say things they could never tell their mothers, girlfriends, sisters. We wondered sometimes how it would be for them, going back with their heads full of things they couldn't tell a soul. Although we knew that most of them would not be going back at all.

In those days our feet hurt and our backs ached and we were always tired, we learned to live with that. In the evenings there was sometimes a dance and after our long day's work we'd be in a truck, bouncing down a dark, rutted road, pulling up in front of a hut or hall packed with men. Hundreds of men and five or six of us and we danced and a whistle blew every few minutes to change partners and sometimes there were vicious fights and we saw that too. How for the space of a dance we were not ourselves, just something everyone wanted to get their hands on. And it made us feel differently about the sweet-faced boys who said we were so like their sisters and we talked about that back in our rooms, pulling off our painful shoes, and we wondered what happened to men in groups, wondered if the war was like that.

In those days most of us fell in love, with each other or with a man in a uniform. Often it was the first time, sometimes the only one. Sometimes it ended happily but usually not. Often they were killed and that became a small hard lump of tragedy that never went away. Sometimes we knew about the wives back home but usually not and when we found out we felt such fools. We were very young; it never occurred to us that people would behave that way. Some of us went too far, snuck away on a weekend pass and met up in a station miles away, two days in a cold room with dingy curtains. If it was discovered — and it usually was, people are always moving in a war, always popping up where you least expect it — we were sent home in disgrace and the shame of that was another hard thing we carried the rest of our lives.

More often in those days young men fell in love with us, especially in those canteens in the camps, the only woman with a thousand men. We pretended we didn't know but we did, of course we did. Sometimes we used it to get things we needed, extra supplies, more wood for the fire, good behaviour. It taught us things about men we were sorry to have to learn.

In those days some of us counted things. The number of steps to the *métro*. The number of buttons in a jar, waiting to be sewn on. The number of times a hand grazed a human hand, doling hot drinks. The number of coins in a pocket, the number of crosses in a field.

In those days there was often an *alerte* at night and we had to go down to the cellar and some of us slept in our clothes because it could happen two or three times. And if we were out in the dark streets we had to look for the blue glowing light, the closest *abri*, and hope that there was room for us. And those were often the worst times, down there in the gloomy cellars, and we found ourselves noticing things strangely and sometimes we found ourselves noticing ears and we realized that not once in our lives had we thought about ears, how individual they are. The flat, round ears of a child on his mother's lap, the big sticking-out ones of the man in the waiter's jacket. Women with long lobes or almost none, some with earrings, some without. We thought very hard about ears, waiting for the bugle to sound, but still we couldn't help wondering, Is this how I'm going to die? Right here, with all these strangers?

\* \* \*

In those days some of us bought ridiculous hats.

In those days the sun did shine sometimes and if we were in Paris we treated ourselves to lunch at Maxim's, at Prunier's. Or drank coffee at a little table outside the Café de la Paix, where everyone we knew was bound to appear before the afternoon was over. And our friends were wittier than anyone we'd ever known, and we ourselves made clever jokes, something we'd never been known for. After the coffee spilled someone wedged a matchbox under a table leg and we laughed and laughed and looking at the swept-clean sky, at the blaze of flowers in the market across the way, it seemed like the only place to be. But even there, at the edge of our vision, were the women and children all dressed in black.

In those days some of us went to the Gare du Nord after work to help with the refugee trains. And we didn't know what was worse, the bewildered old people or the children or the mothers with limp babies in their arms. Sometimes there would be a little boy with a blue cap, standing alone in the middle of all that noise and confusion. His hands at his stomach, clasped tightly around a carved wooden animal, a horse or a cow, maybe; it was roughly carved, and the boy only held on tighter when we asked if he would show us. And we knew that someone had carved it for him, a father or grandfather, sitting on a back step in the sun or beside the fire on a winter evening. It would have become the boy's favourite thing, he would have carried it everywhere, talked to it before he went to sleep, told it all his secrets. When we bent down to him, put an arm around his shoulders, we could feel his whole body trembling, and we walked him to the big red cross, and though we tried and tried we never found out what happened to him after that.

In those days some of us were too tired to sleep and we lay in a cold, dark room and that was when we saw our families' faces.

And we thought of a day spent reading by a rain-soaked window, the tinkle of silver spoons on saucers; we tried to picture ourselves at the dinner table with our short hair and our cigarettes, our opinions. And we knew that we could never go back to being dutiful daughters and we wondered how we could ever go back at all. We thought of our innocent selves then, with great tenderness.

In those days we were all very young, although we felt older than we ever could have imagined.

In those days we never would have guessed that there would be a man with a beard and a tape recorder. That he would lean forward in a shaft of winter sunlight and say, Do you remember anything about the war?

# By the Sea, by the Sea

Each physician should counsel those over whom he has advisory charge of the dangers incident to a prolonged exposure in the ocean.
— *British Medical Journal*, 1904

… and on Tuesday I called on the poor McIntyres, whose daughter Mary died of overbathing last summer in Ostend.
— W. Lumsden, *Rambles through the Shires*, 1906

You have probably seen photographs of Mary McIntyre, you may even have one on the wall in your den, in a box under the stairs. Sometimes she stands at the back, one hand resting on someone's shoulder, or sometimes she sits beside others on a settee, staring straight ahead. She's the one you can't imagine smiling, although in fact she had a lovely smile.

Her clothes are unremarkable. You can't see the colours, of course, but they are usually shades of brown and beige, often different shades in the same dress. Her mother has always preferred brown and she chooses the fabric; it has never really occurred to her that the tones she loves may not be the best for Mary, whose hair is the colour of tea with not enough milk. It looks darker in the photographs. Drawn back smoothly, making her face look even rounder, and her eyes appear dark too, although they were really a flat bluish-grey.

Unless you looked very closely you probably would not notice that her left shoulder is a little higher than the right, the result of a slightly twisted spine, perhaps an accident of birth. Half an inch higher, say, which does not sound like much, which does not even look like much when you bring out the old wooden ruler from your desk drawer. But it was a lot for Mary McIntyre; it may explain everything about Mary McIntyre. Or it may explain nothing at all, it may be incidental and have nothing to do with the things that happened. But someone should understand, or try to. Someone should know about Mary McIntyre and how she looked in that long dress. Someone should know about that summer in Ostend, and the way she vanished from the pictures.

The crossing was rough and her mother's head ached and there was trouble with the luggage and her father had to make a scene, even though he hated to, because it was so often the only way. Afterward he went out walking to calm himself and her mother rested and Mary McIntyre sat in a chair by her open window, listening to the soft *shush* of the sea and trying to make out its oily black surface by the light of the stars. And perhaps she thought about a new place, a new start, or perhaps that never occurred to her. She was a dreamer, something you wouldn't have guessed from her rather heavy, round face, her flat eyes, and often in her dreams she sat just so in a sunny garden, or walked a sandy path, carrying her bonnet by the strings in one hand. In the house where she grew up every sneeze made her mother flinch, every bump or scrape would have her in bed with blankets and potions, a cool hand on her forehead testing for fever. Perhaps she learned it early, this retreat into dreams. Or perhaps it was always her way.

Things might have been different if the others had lived. It was never easy for her mother; her father heard the screams, pacing downstairs or out in the street, and wondered what kind of brute would come to a woman again after that. He tried, he did try, but the tiny stones were planted in the churchyard one by one until Mary lived a year and then two and they began to believe that she was real. Not quite whole, perhaps, although they never would have said, even to each other. The slight curve in her spine that caused pain, from time to time, and the way she was — not simple, not that, but somehow removed. She could read and write and figure, she could learn anything if she put her mind to it, but she didn't often try and to keep her attention fixed on a piece of sewing, a little polite conversation, was next to impossible. At times she said the most peculiar things. A stranger would notice it, a number did that summer at Ostend, but her parents gave no sign.

So here they are at breakfast the next morning, Mother a little pale but otherwise recovered and Father rubbing his hands together before picking up his fork and Mary McIntyre saying that she will not, after all, go into the sea that day.

She doesn't know why she has said it. Her father raises his eyebrows and says, Very well, and she knows that he will talk about the weather a little, and perhaps remark that the dining room is not so crowded at this hour. And then he will mention the cloudless sky again, and say that they have come here so that she can bathe and take the sea air, and then he will pause so that she can explain, but she won't be able to explain. Perhaps it is a premonition, or perhaps a dream she had once and in that dream she reached out a hand under water and someone turned to her very slowly; she saw the face and woke herself screaming. Although no one came running, so perhaps the screaming stayed inside the dream.

She knows that they have come here for her, rather than to Margate or Lowestoft like other years, and she knows that it is only partly for the sea air. More to avoid those familiar faces who ask after her aunt and uncle, who cluck their tongues over poor Charlie and enquire after her own health, having heard something of her collapse. Perhaps her parents are also tired of being reminded but she does not really think of that, so bound is she by her strange, dreamy pain, so used to the way they take care of her. So certain that this rift in the family, the empty places at the holiday table, are all her fault.

Everyone thought it was the first time. The shrieks and loud voices in the attic, the closed door of her room. They didn't know — did they know that it had been going on for years?

Charlie saying, Can we go and play? and her mother's face smiling at where they stood, her aunt too, saying, Run along now, off you go. The way she longed to step into their safe world, to take one step over the drawing-room threshold, and the way she knew it was impossible to do that. Their distant smiling faces in the steam from the silver pot and Charlie tugging at her hand, drawing her off to the garden, the shed, the attic.

This is what people do, Charlie said, although he had only the haziest of notions. Pictures in those books hidden behind the shelves in his father's study. Mary McIntyre's poor pale flesh was nothing like that, but she kept still like he told her and after a time he discovered that it was better if he hurt her a little. How did her mother not notice, rubbing different oils over her crooked back? Even in the flickering light she must have seen the bruises on arms and thighs, in the hollows of collarbones. Charlie saw them himself sometimes, and felt a little ashamed and more than a little amazed at his power. Once he gave her some sweets, flecked with lint from his pocket.

When they were discovered Mrs McIntyre felt her hands go cold and she looked at her brother, his face transformed by rage and the flick in his eye when he caught hers and looked immediately away, so fast that only her icy hands told her she'd really seen it.

She'd never told a soul about those times he held her down, the pain and his sweaty boy-smell, but in that flick of the eye she almost screamed at his whiskered face, the cake crumbs on his vest, the pale napkin still clutched in one hand. Just for a moment and then she heard herself speaking calmly but no one else seemed to, the bluster and the noise and Mary weeping, Charlie cuffed out of the house and down the street, her sister-in-law gasping into her handkerchief.

Things might have been different then. Marooned in her room Mary McIntyre slept and slept, yet still somehow felt she was waking. Until Charlie was sent to a new school where he took diphtheria and quickly died; then some horror knocked her from her feet and rolled her about without mercy. Months passed that are lost to her now although their story may be hidden in the lines around her mother's mouth, the dark bruises that will remain beneath her eyes for the rest of her life.

Someone should know about Mary McIntyre and how she felt that first morning after breakfast, for of course she did go to bathe; there was never really any question. Her parents waited on the shore, sitting straight in their little rented chairs, and someone should have heard her teeth chatter as she pulled on her costume, known the smell of wet wood and dried salt and the shock that went through her at the first touch of the cold hand of the sea, the cold licking tongues of the sea, welcoming her back. She'd been to the seaside before, of course, and paddled for hours when she and Charlie were children. Every year their families holidayed in Folkestone, in Lowestoft or Margate. By the time she was old enough to look forward to things they were getting ready to change, but there were still a few years when Charlie looked after her well, tipping a bucket to make a sand tower, helping her to stand when she had fallen, although he was only half a head taller himself.

In those days it was always hot and clear and she remembers people sitting around a table and her father's moustache moving as he says that you couldn't get better weather anywhere, not even in the tropics. The men swam every morning and the children splashed at the water's edge and even her mother once took off her stockings and clenched her toes in the sand. The end of an afternoon, holding Charlie's sticky hand, grains of sand rubbing between their fingers. The sun still warm on the top of her head for she carries her bonnet by its strings and no one tells her that she must put it on. Her father and uncle walk in front, their shirt sleeves rolled up, and her mother and aunt come behind, holding on to each other and laughing at something, perhaps the way their feet keep slipping. In a moment

she and Charlie will say that their legs are tired and their
fathers will bend down from their great height and swing them
up through the air. But it is the moment just before this that she
recognizes in some way. The hot sun, waves, the faint sound of
a band playing somewhere and the tall, gentle shapes sur-
rounding; it is this moment that hovers at the edge of all her
dreams.

So it cannot be the novelty of the sea that explains what happened that summer, and not the seaside either. A foreign one,
it's true, but one large hotel is much like another, and the promenade, the pier. Differences perhaps in the sanitary arrange-
ments, but even these are not so great. And the sound of
French, of German and even Flemish, but as her mother
remarked last time at Margate, with the babble of accents one
might as well have been in a foreign country.

What was it then that made everything seem strange, and
strangely charged? Perhaps she was changing, Mary McIntyre
that is, perhaps she was on the verge of some great stepping
out. Perhaps if death had not stepped in she would have
clasped her life, and run with it. Or perhaps it was oily Death
all the time, sidling closer, nudging her shoulders, her chest,
twining round. Perhaps that was the thing that coloured it all.

Someone should know about Mary McIntyre, and yet it's so
hard to keep her in focus. Her outline blurs, as it does in those
photographs, as she herself faded out. The sound of her voice
no more than a murmur against the tinkling of silver spoons on
saucers, the competing bands from the park, the pier, from the
great hall of the Kursaal. It becomes harder and harder to know
her first thoughts as she comes awake in the mornings, to know
her mind in the dining room as she cuts carefully at her meat
while the fair-haired waiters move soundlessly from table to
table. The midday sun darts now and then through the high
windows, sparking on cutlery already polished to gleaming,

and it strikes the lines around her father's eyes, the cords in the thinning neck above his collar and she sees that he is growing old, that perhaps he will die soon and that even then things will not really change. She will trail behind her mother forever, from place to place, in and out of season, and the thought makes her incredibly weary, leaves her suddenly without the strength to lift her fork to her mouth.

Across the table her father works his tongue at a bit of gristle lodged in his back teeth; as far as he is concerned foreign meat is always suspect, although he keeps this conviction to himself. He is a decent, baffled man who fears he has misstepped somewhere. He suddenly thinks of bells and white clouds and his wife's hand on his arm and remembers that he felt ready to take on the world. Now the sunlight through the windows is uncomfortably warm; he watches his daughter dreaming, her fork halfway to her lips, and wonders how he could have forgotten to do that.

Mrs McIntyre is also uneasy about the meat, but supposes that she will get used to it. She is a woman of hidden but strong opinions who should have had more to organize than a small household, rounds of visiting, occasional excursions in season. Who might have, in fact, if all those gravestones hadn't battered the life out of her, left her watching her living child, dreaming again, with a helpless mixture of love and despair. Mary's hair pulled back smoothly, covering her ears which fold out a little at the top, just like her father's, her face inclined to plumpness without the bloom of health and her awkward mouth, again so like her father's that her mother can't help thinking of all those small bodies, how one or two had thatches of her own dark hair, how things might have been different.

She stops those thoughts though, just as she stops the pang she feels at the sight of her own mottled hand, reaching out to take a roll from the basket. The rolls are fresh and slightly warm; everything here is as it should be and the waiters anticipate every need without intruding. This is the only way she knows to keep chaos at bay. Breakfast and a stroll, luncheon and a rest, perhaps a concert in the evening. Life can proceed in a strange hotel much as it does at home. She knows that only marriage will be the saving of her daughter and the sight of her own hand suggests that it is not too soon to think about that, to make the acquaintance of some of those mothers whose sons trail, reluctantly or attentively, through the reading room, the picture gallery.

Looking at her husband, his cheek bulging as he works at his teeth, she counts her blessings. She would have done anything to get away from the house where she lived under the shadow of her brothers, and sometimes under their weight. And it was just luck, really, that her husband was still as he had seemed when she first met him — a kind, serious man who took care of things but rarely interfered. He would agree, she is sure, that it is time to think about Mary's future, to think about committing her to someone else's care. And perhaps, in one way of thinking, a European would be quite suitable. Less likely to remark the long silences, the occasional blurting out of the strangest things. And that business with Charlie — but she stops that thought as quickly as it flashes in her mind. She does, however, permit herself a brief dream of some years hence. A courtly son-in-law and the soft curls of grandchildren, the way they smell when she hugs them close.

As it turned out none of that happened and Mrs McIntyre herself was dead within the year, so the dreary round of days that Mary foresaw would not have come to be either. Although it might have, if she herself hadn't stepped from the picture. The final shape determined by each piece slotting in in a particular way, a particular order.

What happened next will be recorded in a stack of dusty records somewhere, a chance combination of streams and currents that comes, once or twice a century, to the coast around

Ostend. The air remained cool but the sea became warmer and warmer and seemed to deepen its colour, the blues and greens as intense as jewels. The breeze on the shore carried the faintest hint of spice, and a barely perceptible rattling, clacking sound. And while her parents sat up straight on the beach in their rented chairs, Mary McIntyre gave herself to the sea again and again. It rolled her around, it rolled around her, she paddled in the shallow warm water and even ducked right under, pulling herself clumsily at first with her arms, her struggling feet, but finally opening her eyes and seeing many things clearly.

Back on the shore where her parents wait it grows crowded and noisy, hawkers everywhere. Her father wishes he'd brought his pipe; he'd thought about it but assumed there would be too much wind, too much trouble fumbling with matches and tobacco. There is a wind, of course, but a mild one, just whispering over his cheek, barely ruffling the sleeve of his wife's dress. They have marked the position of their daughter's ochre-coloured machine and a good thing too, for after an hour the sea is dotted with them and several are a similar shade. He pulls out his watch and remarks that the driver is over time again, not knowing that the driver is quite content to tarry if someone slips him a half franc along with the bathing-coupon. Mrs McIntyre says that she supposes that a few extra minutes won't matter, and that the bathing seems to be doing a world of good, Mary's complexion clearer and her back hasn't ached for days. And meeting her husband's eyes she smiles and he does too, until a newspaper vendor taps him on the shoulder, offering yet another copy of *La Chronique*.

Someone should know about Mary McIntyre and what she thought or sensed, looking out on that vast expanse of scented sea. Looking out toward Margate as she had looked out from Margate, looking out on herself looking out and knowing that she was different. If she cupped her hands round her eyes and looked through she could have been the last person in the world, or the only one, and if she had thought about it she would have been surprised that this didn't frighten her. Quite the opposite, in fact.

When her extra time was up she left her costume in a heap, her stockings sticking a little as she pulled them on because she hadn't taken time to dry properly, so eager was she, in those first few days, to open the door and step out, to carry it all with her into the world.

The mothers had arranged for her to walk the Digue with Gaston in the afternoon, and so they strolled with other couples, with families and groups of girls and young men. Gaston stroked his spotty moustache and spoke of his delicate health, the many treatments taken, and he recited some verses he was proud of, but allowed that perhaps they suffered in English. It was very warm; perspiration beaded the sides of her nose, her upper lip, and Gaston ran a finger beneath his collar. Looking out at the rows of bathing machines she remarked that they were just like people really, and he wrinkled his pale brow.

And as they walked on she felt impatience building until she could have screamed with it. To feel this unyielding surface beneath her feet. To be hearing about Gaston's frail constitution when she felt herself bursting with good health, with luck. She thought of those walks taken with her mother for as long as she could remember. The creak of the gate, the quiet prayers, the two tears that crept down her mother's cheeks. Sometimes it surprised her that there were only two, and sometimes that there were still two. But she had not joined those tiny mounds in the churchyard; she had survived and she felt that now as a triumph instead of a monstrous error.

Someone should know about Mary McIntyre and the way she closed her eyes for a moment, breathing in, hearing the sighing water, the far-off voices and the closer call of seabirds. Feeling the way her heart slowed down, her rough edges smoothed out.

That morning they had gone to the lace market in the Place d'Armes, her father slipping away immediately to the reading room in search of an English newspaper. Her mother and Gaston's made slow progress through the market, stopping frequently to exclaim and rub things between their fingers. And Gaston remained stubbornly by her side, carrying a few packages and fumbling for his white handkerchief. Out of sight of the water she was dazed, she hardly heard a word he said. Straining for the sound of the waves, for the call of those wheeling birds. She began to realize that it had become an urgent thing, that some balance had shifted so slyly that she hadn't even noticed when it had happened. Harsh sunlight bounced back from the buildings lining the square and loud voices and laughter beat at her ears. She tried to call on whatever the sea had given her, that ease in her manner that made her mother smile and pat her hand, that sense of becoming that made each new day a welcome thing. But it had gone, it was gone, and she was left a jagged shell in a hard-edged world, not knowing if she would scream or weep.

So she says some words to Gaston, she doesn't even know what words, and turns and walks quickly away from the square, from the town, walking faster and faster until she hears only the rasping slide of her soft shoes. Gaston starts after her but she moves so quickly, he hasn't really heard what she said, perhaps she is ill, he looks back to where he last saw his mother, searches for her lavender hat, looks back to see the flick of Mary McIntyre's brown skirt as she disappears round a far corner, and coughs briskly into his white handkerchief, wondering what to do.

At luncheon she explained that she had suddenly felt ill, that the bathing had restored her and she was fine now, only a little tired. Later, her mother placed her silver brush on the dressing-table and said that she supposed that it was all right, and her father said that he thought Gaston a poor sort of fellow anyway.

And they agreed that she was getting older, that perhaps they should let go a little, and they agreed that the bathing seemed to make her happy and that, after all, was what they had come here for. After that Mary McIntyre went down to the beach twice a day and sometimes more and the drivers began to watch out for her, and her extra half franc. On the promenade her mother took her father's arm and he bent his head, in his courtly way, to hear something she had said.

The sea stayed warm and it was warmer on shore now and they all rested in the afternoon. Gaston and his mother returned to Liege where he would soon meet the pale woman who would become his first wife. He will bury her and two others, clutching his white handkerchief in a changing world, and as an old man he will come back to Ostend to consult another specialist, will sit in a waiting room in a stray shaft of sunlight and wonder at his sudden unease, at the thought that things could have been different. Then someone will call his name and he will stop trying to remember whatever it is that he has forgotten.

And Mary McIntyre slept without resting, moaned and kicked in the underwater light of her room, the green shutters closed against the afternoon sun. Her appetite dwindled and a doctor, strolling past her on the terrace with his hands clasped behind his back, might have noticed, fleetingly, the light in her eyes, the colour in her face. The air was warm and one day, hurrying to dress for dinner, she opened her wardrobe and caught a glimpse of blue between the brown and beige sleeves and pulled out a shimmering dress like nothing she had ever seen. The way it fell about her, the ripples of colour like deep water splashed with sunlight; her hands trembled as she hooked it up.

In the dining room she thanked her mother and talked on and on, her eyes sparkling and her cheeks flushed. Raising the fork to her lips and putting it down, untasted. And across the table Mrs McIntyre felt a cold hand at her heart and knew that this was what she had been waiting for.

If someone had seen Mary McIntyre in that blue dress things might still have been different. If someone had held out a human hand, even then, she might have known at once the truth about the soft fingers of the sea. But no one did. The dining room was full, people talked and laughed quietly over the faint sound of the waves outside the dark windows. The fair-haired waiters stepped softly between the tables, their thoughts far away in their own country. Each piece fitted where it did, creating the perfect space for the one that came after, and the one after that. And some time during the night the sly currents shifted, rolled back to slide onto white sand shores, beneath chattering palms. By morning she was delirious with fever; they sent for Dr Garnier, who shook his head, and then there was nothing left but the watching and waiting.

Someone should know about Mary McIntyre, but no one ever will. She remains as remote, as mysterious as the person who sits next to you on the crowded bus, brushes past you on a busy street. Even someone who was right there could only guess at the things she dreams on the ochre-coloured steps, in her rumpled bed, the things she goes on dreaming. Dreaming the beach at Ostend, a cool wind brushing her cheeks, combing through her loosened hair. Dreaming the wild smell of the sea, the cries of spinning birds. Dreaming that her life will go on and on, that she will be there until the story ends.

# The New Wife

The old wife was there at the beginning. She wears her hair in an outdated style, she is trapped in her black-and-white life between the pages of a book that hasn't been opened for years. A small, glossy photo with a serrated white edge, a date in black, one crumpled corner. She looks so young.

The new wife is much older, of course. They live in a house that is new to both of them and their faces are tanned most of the year from the things they do, the places they go. The old wife loved the beach and shook sand out of her hair on holidays. She loved to swim too, to become a tiny dot looking back at the shore. One night she swam away.

The old wife was there even before the first child and she was the one who placed her in his arms, all three of them touching. It was early morning; breakfast trays rattled and autumn trees blazed against a cold blue sky. He doesn't think much about the weather now, but the old wife brings it with her every time. Hot sun on the top of his head, the *clock* of the windshield wipers on a drive to the airport. The sweat between her breasts and the smell of melting asphalt through a wide open window. For some reason he thinks of a summer night, dense and humid, filled with the sound of insects. He stands with one hand on the refrigerator, the floor almost cool beneath his feet, and the old wife sits in a circle of light at the kitchen table and that light gleams on her hair, so exactly the colour of the hair of the second child, standing at her shoulder. She is astonished, the old wife, and she tells the child that she didn't know that about sea otters, that she thinks it wonderful that she has lived so long, not knowing, while he in such a short time has come upon this fact. They are talking to each other in a circle of light and neither one turns their gleaming head at the sound of the refrigerator door opening.

The new wife was a widow whose husband was in the same line of work; she came with her own car. He had met her a number of times over the years and he thinks of that sometimes with mild surprise, watching her put on lipstick in the little mirror in their front hall. Or when she holds his arm for balance as she reaches to untie a golf shoe. She has known him only as the successful man he is, unlike the old wife who tied his tie before his first job interview, who washed his sweat-stained shirt. Who held his forehead more than once, in his youth, while he retched over a toilet bowl.

Sometimes the old wife sat in a chair by the window all day, holding a baby and watching the falling snow. Coming home in the early dark he saw their haloed shapes and paused with one hand on the car door, something happening in his chest. There was also a time when the old wife sat by the window all day with a glass in her hand, but that was another thing entirely.

The old wife had a temper; sometimes she yelled and cried and threw things, because sometimes there were things that mattered that much. Once when he came home late he realized that he had forgotten some occasion, some event. All three of them standing facing him, winter coats and boots on, like a wall he had to break through.

The new wife has a lot to say about this and that, but she doesn't have to say it all to him. She had a life already, has hobbies and routines, a network of friends. At first he made an effort to keep them straight, to show an interest, and found that it wasn't actually much of an effort. That he was — not interested maybe, but involved. She is remarkably even-tempered, and hums in the mornings as she opens all the curtains. If she has moments of darkness he has yet to see one, and even the occasional spats within her group are quickly resolved.

After the old wife swam away he hired housekeepers, even when the children had gone. He worked hard in those years to expand his business, to spread his name, to become known as a man who got things done. And he felt as if he was expanding too, as if he could be the man he was, as if he could do anything at all. He did all that and still made sure that his children didn't suffer for it. He applauded at sporting events, took pictures at graduations, gave advice. As adults they seem to be neither more nor less confused or unhappy than the children of people he knows.

The old wife had the best of the children; he believes that. Oh, the sleepless nights, the mess and the worry, but also those times when only she would do. The feeling of tiny hands clasping at the back of her neck. She said once that she felt as if her job was done, but he didn't understand what she meant.

For the new wife, his children are already the people they have become, the bold outlines on a plain white ground. The man with the trim beard, the soft stomach and the red sports car. The sharp-tongued daughter whose hair is suddenly half grey. It's not surprising; she's old enough to have children of her own almost grown. But he wonders if the old wife would have gone that way too. Wonders, sometimes, what the third child would have been like.

The new wife raises funds for things, good things, and he occasionally finds himself in a straw boater and striped jacket, selling raffle tickets. She is always packing up boxes for rummage sales and he jokes sometimes that she is giving away his old life, that what his children didn't take, she is getting rid of. He jokes sometimes that she is paring them down, that she won't be satisfied until they're left with only a mat for sleeping and eating, that he should never have taken her to Japan that time. In Tokyo the new wife bought silky, shimmering things in rich colours that didn't suit her at all. They billowed when she turned before the mirror, and he wondered what she saw. The old wife would have hated the city, but she would have loved the mist on the green hills. The dainty knees of the children walking with satchels strapped to their backs.

There is not much left of the old wife. Her name inside the front cover of a few books, a flicker in the way his children laugh or move their heads, as sudden and startling as the sting of a wasp. The book the photograph fell from was an old geometry text and as he slots it into the box he remembers learning that when a line is continued on into the infinite to the right, it returns again from the left. There are things that nag at him now, little details he finds himself trying to remember, things the old wife would know. The name of the woman with the gap in her teeth, the colour of the upholstery in their first car. The look on his daughter's face on the morning of her sixth birthday, when she opened the back door and saw the red bicycle, sunlight sparking off its spokes.

That humid night, much later, he asked the old wife what it was about sea otters. She was almost asleep; Nothing, she said, it was nothing. But what, he said, and she said it was just something the boy had read in a book. But *what*, he said and his voice got louder because at that moment it was something he had to know. And she gave a huge sigh and shifted her body; it was dark, but he could tell she wasn't looking at him. She told him that sea otters ate while floating on their backs, that they could use their stomachs as a table or as a hard surface to crack open something with a shell. That they did this, as the boy had explained, because they spent most of their life in water, and hardly ever came to land.

Now you tell me, the old wife said out of the dark. You tell me which thing came first.

# On the Border

It was a hot day. He was killing chickens for all the old women and the knife was sticky and terrible. He threw each severed bird to the ground where it jerked and beat its wings, and when it was still a woman lifted it by one taut foot, holding it well away from her body. Dark splatters held down the dust, in places. The other women stood together, shaded by the brims of their floppy hats, talking about children and grandchildren. And noticed, suddenly, that he lay face down in the dust and the blood and the feathers, not moving. For a terrible moment it seemed that he had cut his own throat, by mistake.

And then everything else was moving, everyone running; they turned him over and a foreign girl tried to make him breathe. She plucked a curled white feather from his chin before she covered his mouth with her own. The women's voices twittered above her head and their splattered shadows bobbed and swooped at the edge of her vision. The tip of a long blond braid brushed his empty eyes. She saw that her hand had left a dusty streak across his face and she wanted to stop and wipe it off, but the nurse came and the ambulance, and they drove away in a great hurry although they knew there was no point. He was an old man, not given to troubling anyone; he died without a sound.

When they told his wife two women stood to catch her as she fainted, as they had expected she would. They were in the laundry room; they eased her on to a pile of waiting sheets and dabbed her face with water from a sprinkler bottle. A large-bladed fan circled slowly over their heads. They straightened her thick glasses and led her to her room, one on either side and several behind. It was very quiet. They passed a man and a young boy digging in a garden, spades whispering through the dry earth.

It was a hot day, but the room was dark and cool. When they opened the front door the first thing they saw was his slippers, side by side, waiting to be stepped into, and they thought she might faint again, but she didn't. They stayed with her through the long afternoon, speaking of all their losses, husbands and sons. Her neighbour, coming home, slipped through the net of hidden voices, feeling the handle of the door suddenly cool and smooth in his hand. His wife brushed out her long blond hair, and they lay down to sleep.

Later, the widow began to wail and cry out loud. Next door the girl woke and turned to her husband; he lay on his back, lips slightly parted, and she closed her eyes against his sleeping mouth. On the other side of the wall someone told Leah to take a pill, and there was quiet.

The daughters arrived with the last bus from Jerusalem, late in the night. They spoke softly, made coffee and tea. One dropped a spoon and giggled like a child at the sudden sound. They walked about in their hard-soled shoes for hours and their footsteps echoed, as in an empty house.

All the next day the widows came and went, carrying plates of biscuits and cakes, different soups. They walked her in front of the house, one cupping an elbow on either side. She was smaller than any of them.

In the late afternoon they carried Yoav down the winding road to the cemetery, near the river. Some of the men had just come from the fields and red dust coated their shoes, legs. Leah moved like a sleepwalker between her two tall daughters. Her eyes, behind the thick lenses, were very pale, and her feet barely marked the ground. The place was ringed with eucalyptus trees, grown tall, and long wild grasses, bamboo. To the east, the dusty hills of a hostile country. His friends made short speeches as the shadows crept in. They put Leah in a car with her daughters, and it was finished.

It was hot. August, the killing time. The floors of the rooms were tiled, smooth, and all the shutters were kept closed. Primitive air conditioners hummed and the rooms were dim and almost cool. So hard to open a door and step outside, in August. To step into light so bright; even the flowers, violent reds and yellows, attacked the eyes. To open a door and step outside, feel the heat wrapping around the body, sweat forming in the places between fingers, in every tiny crease. Every day the sun stabbing down from a hard blue sky; it had been so for months, every day as bad as the day before. Late in the afternoons a teasing breeze rattled the branches of palm trees, a warm breeze that died almost as it began. And always the night fell down, thick and still; nothing moved. People fought with their friends and punished their children, fell from ladders and tangled their hands in machinery. People stretched tighter and tighter, in August.

Leah came back from visiting with her daughters and said that someone had been in her room. She stood in her neighbours' kitchen, kneading her fingers, one by one.

'You didn't hear anything?' she said. 'You didn't see anything? Ask Allon when he comes home, maybe he knows.'

'It's very odd,' Allon's wife said, later. 'The key was with her, someone must have an extra key. The lock wasn't forced, I looked.'

'Did they take anything?' Allon said, unbuttoning his shirt, running his hands through his dusty hair.

'That's also strange,' she said, 'they took strange things. An umbrella. Some old records. A wooden spoon. And she said that Yoav's clothes were all messed up, but she didn't think that anything was missing.'

'Tell her to speak to Ezra,' Allon said. 'Tell her to get him to change the lock.'

'I already did,' his wife said.

'Then that should be the end of it.'

Later, when the long shadows stretched across the grass, he walked with Leah through the garden at the side of her room.

'Yoav took care of it,' she said. 'I don't know anything about it.'

So Allon walked with her through the garden and named each plant. He told her when to water, and exactly how much, although she didn't seem to be listening.

'It's a nice garden,' he said. 'Yoav made it very nice.'

But she didn't seem to be listening.

The carpenter came home late and angry, slamming doors.

'Wasting my time,' he said. 'I can't take a step without some old woman wanting something.'

He drank from a bottle of cold water and rammed it back into the refrigerator; it rattled icily beneath his words.

'Nothing wrong with the lock,' he said, 'I've got better things to do. Why would anyone want anything from her anyway?'

His wife studied psychology, from educational television. She said, 'It's natural, she's just lost Yoav, her security. It's symbolic, you see, having the locks changed.'

The carpenter snorted and went to have a cold shower. The water was tepid and he cursed in several languages. His wife looked through the kitchen window and saw herself walking away, with a white flower in her hair and a suitcase in her hand.

The night fell down, heavy and still. Allon's mother, moving through it, passed a lighted window. A young girl crossed a room, holding her heavy hair on top of her head with both hands. Her steps were violent, three strides across the room.

Allon's mother walked faster; she was late for a meeting. But a caged girl paced through her mind.

The meeting-room was thick with cigarette smoke and everyone was tired, and tired of trying to solve everyone else's problems. Typewritten requests stuck to their hands.

'We should talk about what to do with Leah,' Allon's mother said.

'It's very sad,' the younger women said. 'It's always very sad. But she'll get over it, with time.'

Their heads ached and their children were all crying somewhere and their husbands would all be in bed asleep when they got home. Allon's mother said, 'I've known her more than thirty years and she's never been able to get over anything, not without help. I remember when she came here ...'

The younger women sighed and lit more cigarettes. They knew the story, as they knew all the strange sad stories of the past. Grandparents disappearing beyond the range of the high arc lights, orders shouted in a harsh language. Parents jumping from moving trains, hiding in cellars, fighting over mouldy crusts of bread. Leah appearing from the dark hole of Europe, a strange little thing, skittering along the dusty track like a frightened deer. She was somehow not all right, and they wanted to send her away. But Yoav, who never asked for anything, begged them to let her stay, swore that all he wanted in this life was to take care of her. The younger women knew the story, as they knew all those stories of the beginning. Sharing clothes and singing all night, fighting malaria and hacking in the dusty earth for hours. Years. They had heard it all before and they were tired; their heads ached and their eyes scratched and their children were all crying somewhere.

'Why don't we arrange for some course,' the carpenter's wife said. 'Something creative, something — '

'Let's discuss it next time,' someone said. 'It's very late.'

'Next time,' Allon's mother said.

Walking home she thought of her second husband. Killed by a sniper's bullet, down by the border. The day they were married the sky filled with strangely shaped clouds and they tried to read their future. They bought a sack of peanuts to share with the others, and began to eat them, walking down the dusty road from town. Strange, but after thirty years the sound of her footsteps is the splintering of their shells. She can feel a dusty powder on her fingertips, almost taste them on her tongue.

Leah washed the front step, over and over. She thought she saw footprints, creeping to her front door, and no matter how many times she scrubbed and washed, they were there to lead her in.

Allon's blond wife peeled onions in the main kitchen. She sat on a low wooden chair; all around her giant steam pots hissed and women shouted and banged heavy metal dishes. She recited a poem in her own language; something from school, a long time before. A pine bough, caressed by falling snowflakes. Tears slipped from her eyes. The onions, she said. Later she fainted and the women stroked her hot face and sent her home. Onion tears pressed at her eyes the whole way and she almost ran when she saw the front door. She splashed her face with cold water, holding it with her cupped hands. Kjerstin, she said. My name is Kjerstin and I come from a place where it snows, in winter, and you can read your words in the clear air.

'Kjerstin,' a voice said. 'Kjerstin, are you there?'

It took her some moments to realize that the voice came from outside, that Leah was scrabbling at the door, wanting in.

'Look,' Leah said, standing in the open doorway, reaching into the pocket of her faded dress. 'Look, he's still getting in.'

She held out a silver pen in a hard plastic case. Fiery needles danced, straight to Kjerstin's eyes.

'It's not the same pen,' Leah said. 'Yoav gave it to me, for a present. My name was engraved on it. Someone took it, and put another in its place.'

'What kind of person would do that,' Leah said, turning away, letting the door close slowly.

'I think there's something wrong,' Kjerstin said. 'I think there's something very wrong.'

She set a tray on a low table and sat down, her knee touching her husband's. 'No one would do that, why would anyone do that? And last week she said that one of Yoav's undershirts was missing. She's not all right.'

'Of course she's not,' Allon said. 'Her husband's suddenly dead and she's all alone.

'What would you do,' Allon said, dropping a match into an ashtray just before it burned his fingers. 'What would you do if I went off to the army and didn't come back?'

'I wouldn't spend all day counting your undershirts,' she said, and he smiled and spooned too much sugar into his coffee cup.

Allon drove through the fields all day in a rattling jeep. Checking irrigation lines, opening and closing valves, soaked by the foul-smelling river water and steaming dry in the August sun, over and over again. Almost every day he drove past the place where a bullet found his father, and he wondered why on this day he had stopped to think of it.


The border patrol found footprints near the fence, as the sun was going down. The men picked up their guns and went off to guard the perimeter, the children's houses; it happened, from time to time. The static from their radios carried a long way, and orange flares lit the sky.

The carpenter's wife packed a small suitcase and hid it under the bed. She went out into the crackling night to look at her youngest son, who dreamed terrible things. Looking down at his sleeping face she thought that she might weaken, after all, and take him with her.

Allon's mother was translating an article for the newspaper. She spoke five languages easily; before Independence she had walked through dangerous countries in various disguises, setting up escape routes. As a girl of fifteen she had moved through an occupied city, carrying guns in her hollowed-out schoolbooks. Now she lifted her hands from the typewriter and rubbed at her tired eyes, knowing that the shutters were closed. She heard the coloured flares rising, and remembered a night in '48. Remembered sitting alone in a dark room, listening to the pounding of the long guns and letting herself think, for a moment, that they could never survive.

Something scratched at Kjerstin's door, very late.

'Don't be afraid, it's Leah, it's only me.'

She was wrapped in a cotton robe, her hair tumbled, her eyes small and vulnerable without her glasses; Kjerstin couldn't bear to look at her. The same cringing feeling that came when she saw Leah's faded underwear hanging on a line by the front door.

'Everything's dark,' Leah said. 'I plugged in the kettle and everything went out, what should I do?'

'It's probably just a fuse,' Kjerstin said, slipping an old letter between the pages of a book. 'Do you have extra fuses?'

'What do they look like,' Leah said. 'I don't know, Yoav fixed everything, I don't know what to do. Can you go to find someone?'

'Let me try,' Kjerstin said.

Next door in Leah's room it was already stuffy, and very hot. A tall candle burned in the kitchen, the only light. Kjerstin climbed on a chair and began trying fuses. Leah's wild-haired shadow danced on the wall. With the sound of each flare rising she jumped and twitched.

'I hate the noise,' she said. 'I hate that noise. Like the war, like all the wars, with the big guns pounding at night. Yoav is gone and no one can help me now, he'll find me now.'

The fuse connected and the room jumped out at them, but Leah didn't seem to notice. She was staring down at her hands, rubbing her palms together, hard.

'It was an accident,' she said. 'We didn't intend ... he was a little man with broken teeth. We ambushed his truck. We only wanted the petrol, we didn't know what to do with him. We had no place for prisoners, no food for prisoners. He sat on the floor with his hands tied behind his back, crying and shaking, and I said I would shoot him.'

The only sound was the rubbing of her wrinkled hands.

'It's all right,' Kjerstin said softly. 'I've fixed it, Leah, and the noise has stopped and it's not dark any more.'

'Why can't he leave me alone,' Leah said, as she closed the door. As the lock clicked.

When she first came to this place, Kjerstin saw everything. A man wheeling a baby carriage, with a machine gun balanced on top. Concrete bunkers, grown over with flowers and children's paintings. Now when Allon put on his green uniform and disappeared for a few days, a few weeks, she thought only that she would miss him, while he was gone. Nights like this when the sky was bright and anything could happen, she picked up a book and waited to hear that it was over.

It was a hot day and the carpenter came into the dining room angry. He sat down at a table with some friends and said, 'That's it. It's too much. It's craziness, that's all it is.'

His friends said, 'What do you care? Put in a few locks and keep the old woman quiet, what's the problem?'

An old man stood up, pushed in his chair. He was remembering a stormy meeting, near the beginning. Fists crashing on the table, making the coffee cups chatter. And Yoav standing up and saying, in his quiet way, that the day there was a lock anywhere on the kibbutz would be the day he would leave.

'Things change,' the old man said, but no one heard.

The carpenter finished his dinner, smoked a cigarette and felt better. He crossed the cool dining room to tell Leah that he would put small hooks inside all the windows. But he wouldn't change the lock again. It was new, and expensive, and he had other things to do.

Allon's wife wrapped her blond braids about her head and they walked through bright flowers to his mother's room. It was Friday and the place was noisy with children and grandchildren, eating and drinking.

'When did she tell you this?' Allon's mother said.

'The night they shot the terrorists.'

'Ah,' Allon's mother said, as if everything was explained.

'Is it true?'

'I don't know,' Allon's mother said. 'We had prisoners here once or twice, in '48. By accident really. We never killed them, we sent them on as soon as we could, that's all. But Leah was some time on another place, it may have happened there. I doubt it, but who knows. We were all on one border or another, all those years. Things happen, in a war.'

'But she is really frightened,' Kjerstin said. 'She thinks that he's come back for her, she thinks that now that Yoav's gone he's come back for her.'

'Nonsense,' Allon's mother said. 'She's always been afraid of something. Afraid that her children would hurt themselves, playing games. Afraid that there wasn't enough flour and we would all be hungry again. I've discussed it with the health committee; there's really nothing we can do. And she's still working, she still comes to the dining room, actually she's managing better than I thought she would.'

'But she's not,' Kjerstin said.

'Ezra's wife thinks she should take up macramé and find herself,' Allon's mother said.

'Ezra's wife watches too much television,' someone said, and they laughed.

Allon's mother served coffee in glass cups and opened the windows.

'We're all being spoiled,' she said. 'There's nothing so

terrible about a little night air, nothing wrong with being a little uncomfortable. We lived for years without even dreaming of air-conditioning. We survived.'

The August heat oozed into the room. Allon lay on the floor with his two small nephews. They rolled a sponge ball back and forth; tiny bells were sewn inside, a clear, clean sound.

On a hot day Leah climbed three stone steps to ask the security officer for a gun. A small pistol, something. The security officer was washing his hands outside the dining room. He had been up most of the night. His wife was sleeping with his neighbour and his oldest son wore a diamond earring and all he wanted was to be sitting down in a cool room somewhere. He raised his voice and shook water from his hands and Leah ran like a frightened deer.

When the carpenter's wife heard the story that evening she nodded and began to talk about phallic symbolism, but she heard her own voice, suddenly, and stopped.

'Someone should call her daughters,' she said. 'Maybe she needs to get away for a while, maybe she just needs a change.'

'Tell it to the health committee,' Ezra said. 'I'm tired.'

His wife turned out the light, and thought that the summer would never end.

September was a slow, drawn-out sigh. A few white clouds appeared, small but promising. People sat out in the evenings, sipping iced drinks; quiet voices like the rustling of leaves on the trees. The carpenter's wife unpacked her suitcase and Allon's mother began to knit a small white blanket. Leah's old underwear danced on the line, making Allon's wife laugh out loud, although she was by herself. People began to recognize each other and waited for the rain, and the afternoon breeze was a slow, drawn-out sigh.

The prisoner came some time during a cool night. In the

morning one of the widows called, Leah, wake up, it's late. Knocking on the front door. Later she said, I knew, before I even looked inside; it was the sound of an empty house.

It was six o'clock and the grass was still damp; her sandals left faint marks on the tiled floor. The room was murky, only the pale light that slipped through the open window.

Leah sat in a chair in a pale circle of light by the open window. Into the silence came the sound of her quiet breathing. Her glasses lay on the floor beside the chair, and her empty eyes were terrible. They took her away in an ambulance, and no one was particularly surprised.

# Max, 1970

Max's father is teaching him how to fix the dishwasher. It is not going well. Saturday afternoon, a pale dead sky through the kitchen window, through the bare branches of the lilac tree. Something like opera on the radio. Max thinks that any minute now he will have to scream.

It's not like there's anything really wrong with the dishwasher. A low hum at the end of the rinse cycle, a few streaks on the plates and glasses. Surely not enough to merit this savagery, the way it has been disembowelled on the off-white linoleum, wires hanging loose. An open toolbox full of things that have names he can't even guess at.

In the living-room his mother is fitting his sisters' costumes and he can hear them twittering, the occasional squeal when a pin scrapes the skin. He pictures their pigtails flicking against their shoulders. It's Hallowe'en and they're going out as angels — what a joke. Max is tapping his foot on the floor, the frayed bell of his jeans almost covering his running shoe. Three inches away from his father's nose where he's peering at something under the machine and Max knows the tapping will be driving him crazy but he can't stop. He sees the way his father's hair is growing back in strange, tufty patches, nothing like it used to be, and he looks out the window instead. Then up to the clock above it. He was on his way out to the plaza when his father appeared with the toolbox. Typical, the way they're always going on at him about making new friends and then telling him there's some stupid job to be done. With his father home from the hospital he doesn't have to look after his sisters so much, but they just don't understand how things work here.

'Why don't you invite them over to listen to some records,' his mother says in that new cheerful voice she has.

By now they'll all be gathered behind Woolworth's, rolling cigarettes and striking matches on the pale brick. No one will notice that he's not there, and even if they did they wouldn't wonder about it. They'll move on somewhere without him and at the moment this seems incredibly tragic.

'Well, look at this,' his father says suddenly and Max squats down, peering at a mess of wires and trying to see what's caused all the excitement.

'Do you see,' his father says, and Max says, 'Yeah, sure.'

As he stands up there's a sudden jerk and a pain in his scalp that brings tears to his eyes, a chunk of his long hair snagged around a nut or a screw or whatever the damn thing is.

'Oh shit,' he says before he can stop himself, but his father doesn't seem to notice, says, 'What happened? Max — hold still, don't panic. I'll get the scissors.'

'No scissors!' Max shrieks, and as he does there's a sudden memory of a chair in the middle of the kitchen in their old house, the tea kettles on the yellowed wallpaper, his feet swinging off the floor, the buzz of his father's electric clippers.

'Hold still,' his father says, as if he had a choice, and now all Max can see is his father's fingers, gently unwinding. He can't remember ever looking at his father's hands, but he's sure they weren't like this. So pale they're almost greenish, shaking a little. Punctures and bruises on the back from his last hospital stay and Max thinks suddenly that it must hurt. Then he is free, rubbing at his scalp, a few blond strands wrapped tightly around an evil-looking bolt.

'If you'd get a damned haircut that wouldn't happen,' his father says, and Max thumps his feet as he leaves the room. He meets his mother in the hallway and she stops him by putting one hand on his shoulder, he can feel the anger leaving him, as if she's drawing it out with that hand.

'There are just things you have to know, Max,' his father says, back in the kitchen.

'I already know how to use the Yellow Pages,' Max says, but

then he throws up his hands and says, 'Just kidding,' and his father lets it go.

Neither of them has the patience for this, and Max wonders why he's the only one who seems to know it.

While Max puts the tools away his father hooks the dishwasher hose onto the tap. He can hear his sisters bouncing a ball against the wall of the house as his father turns the dial. The low hum is gone, but in its place there's a loud metallic rattle. He looks up sideways from his crouch and sees his father's still back, his right hand reaching slowly to turn the dial again, turn off the tap. He walks from the room, and Max hears the back door close quietly. With a sigh he wheels the dishwasher to the middle of the floor and unscrews the back again, then realizes he has no idea what to do next. Looking through the back door he sees his father sitting on the cold lawn, his knees drawn up to his chest, one hand pulling up little chunks of grass and letting them fall slowly from his grasp. After what seems like a long time Max's sisters appear, running. They throw themselves on their father, wrapping their arms around his neck. Then they all stand up and Max moves away before they turn around.

In the shower he tries a couple of numbers, using the soap as a microphone, but his heart doesn't seem to be in it. He plops the white washcloth on top of his head and folds his lips over his teeth, checking in the hazy shower mirror; his eyes startle him. Then he notices something red and bulging right in the middle of his chin and he peers more closely.

'Oh shit,' he says and hears his sisters gasp outside, the sound of running feet. 'Spies,' he shouts, opening the door and releasing a swirl of steam. 'I'm surrounded by spies!'

It's late when Max arrives at the party and he wanders from room to room, the music pulsing through him. He's covered his face with white makeup, almost sure that the spot on his chin is invisible. Hair slicked back, lipstick blood dripping around his mouth.

'You look sweet,' a girl named Judy says, dancing by.

'I'm *Dracula*, for Chrissake,' he says, but she's already gone.

He keeps walking around until he finds the back door and lets himself out, keeps moving. He walks around the Crescents and the Roads and the Drives, under the cold stars. He misses his friend Rob and the way they used to race their bikes, the way they knew every tree, every blade of grass in town. All the things they never had to say to each other. The letters they write once in a while aren't the same, aren't even worth doing really.

Once, when they were in fourth grade, their teacher pulled the world map down over the blackboard and then showed them a book with maps the explorers had drawn hundreds of years ago. After they'd all laughed at the sizes and shapes she told them to think about how hard it would be to make a map if you didn't already know how the world looked, or if you couldn't look down from a great distance. In the weeks before the moving truck came, Max walked around his town with a mapmaker's eye, memorizing every mound, every secret path. The distance from his doorway to his bed, the exact pattern of the cracks on the ceiling.

Max walks around the side of their little house to the back yard and sits down at the picnic table he should have put away weeks ago. Smokes a cigarette and wonders if his mother will comment on the smell of his clothes. There's no way of knowing what she'll choose to get worked up about these days. As bad as his sisters during supper, thinking she heard someone at the door, stepping over the toolbox as she got up to peek around the corner and coming back, laughing at herself. Fussing about whether she'd bought enough candy.

'Next year I'll have a better idea,' she said, 'it's just all so different here, I don't know what to expect.'

Something in her voice that Max had never heard before, when she was talking to him, something in the tone and the way she met his eyes, like they were on a level.

All around him there are sounds of the neighbourhood shutting down. A garage door closing, the rattle of a garbage can lid. A low whistle and the chinking of a dog's collar. There are things he can't help thinking about. The way his mother's shoes fall by the front door when she pulls them off after work, and how some time later she sets them neatly side by side. The way his sisters with their floating hair really did look like angels. The way his father used to play catch with him long after supper, the way the ball loomed out of the dark in the split second before it smacked into his glove, and how even if they could do that again, it wouldn't be the same. He wants suddenly, desperately, to be any age but what he is, to be anyone else.

His fingers are numb and he flicks his butt over the low hedge, for the people with the Siamese cats to find. His own house is dark except for the neon haze that comes from the top of the stove, the orange light over the back door, glowing to guide him in. He tries to imagine that this moment is long in the past, tries to imagine where he will be, what he will be doing on a Saturday night in October in ten years, in twenty or thirty.

Of all the things he might have considered, he could never have guessed that it would be this. Feeling the thick, humid air of a foreign country as it oozes through an open window, bringing with it the sound of calling voices, of traffic that never stops. Standing on a shaky ladder while a long-haired woman steadies the base. Holding three coloured wires that dangle from a hole in the ceiling, trying frantically to remember something his father once said. Certain that if he gets it wrong the whole world will go up in a blaze of light.

# Emma's Hands

Emma's hands are pudgy now, but once they flailed like tiny stars; once they drifted through air like soft fronds under water. Covered now in nicks from her sharp new teeth, from who knows what. These first tiny wounds I can't protect her from.

Emma's hands are baby hands now, generic, and it's impossible to say whose they resemble. Impossible to guess what her fingers will look like, holding a glass, touching her cheek, adorned with silver rings. But her thumbnail is my father's, broad and flat and quite distinct, appearing also in one sister, another's son. It should be possible to trace that thumbnail back, to trace it like a mouth, like the shape of an eye, like a talent for music. I have tried to do it, photographs spread out on the living room floor while the day fades. While Emma sighs and whispers, lying beneath the faded blanket my own mother made for me. I have tried to do it, but these ancestors keep hands folded in laps or clenched stiffly at their sides, nothing revealed. Is it the nail of Susan, who clutched the rail of the ship and saw an iceberg steal by like a nightmare? The nail of the minister with outrageous whiskers, the nail of hard-eyed Judith who waited for him to come home. The nail of the lawyer who lost his wife, the nail of the grocer who whipped his sons, the nail of the son, dead in a French field. Is it the nail of the husband who gripped a pen between strong fingers, who dipped and wrote, scratching the page, faster and more furiously? Or does it belong to Norah, who opened the letter miles away? The hands of Norah who folded the letter, who folded all the letters, and kept them together in a place where they would be safe for more than a hundred years.

There is a photograph of Norah, middle-aged. Taken against the wall of a house, head and shoulders, enlarged, with a misty blur where the arms should be, cropped off before the hands, which are surely lying clasped in her lap. She might be smiling; her lips are almost smiling, but there is something about the eyes ...

She looks astonishingly like my grandmother, as I knew her. But at the time of the letters my grandmother was not even a thought, speck of a possibility. At the time of the letters there were only the two small boys, and a black hole where Clara had been.

She travelled home by boat and train, a journey that could take three days, a journey that would give her too much time to think. It was August, hot in her layers of black, but there would have been a breeze on the deck of the boat and perhaps she walked there, perhaps she gripped the rail like her great-grandmother, also looking into the vast unknown. She would have prayed; she might have thought of jumping.

She met him after church one day; he had come to visit a distant relative, being in need of a complete change of scene. Or so he told her later in the week when they went out walking in a brisk spring wind. He told her other things, told her about his successful business, the small house in the booming town near the lake. And then he astonished her by suddenly leaping straight into the air to pluck a blossom from an overhanging branch. He landed awkwardly, almost falling, and even while she clapped a hand to her lips she noticed that he somehow maintained his serious air as he stumbled, as he straightened up and offered her the flower with a small bow. In the same way he asked if he might write to her when he returned home, and pressed her hand for a moment when they parted.

'This is the story,' my grandmother said, 'of how my father met my mother.'

'Listen,' my grandmother said, 'because I am the last one, there is no one else who can tell you these things.'

'Listen,' my grandmother said, and I listened. But I also

examined my fingernails, scratched my knee. Thought of the boy with brown eyes who had smiled at me the day before. The tiny apartment was hot, crammed with several lifetimes of furniture, of china. Summer treetops, not moving, through the balcony doors.

'Listen,' my grandmother said, and I thought I did. But now that I have come to this time that she thought of, this time when I would want to know, I find that I have only scraps, and wonder if it is enough. And wonder if she also made her story from bits and pieces, if her mother did, and hers before.

He must have written to her, when he returned home, but she didn't keep those letters. Sitting at his cluttered desk at the back of the store, or late at night in his tidy house he would have told her more about himself, his prospects. He had already decided that they should be married soon after her nineteenth birthday, if she consented. He had arranged to come back at Christmas to speak with her father, and suggested that the ceremony be performed then, to save the trouble and expense of another long journey.

'Oh, love —' her Aunt Fan said, when she asked the question. 'That will come, don't you fret about that.'

So he came at Christmas, and she had thought him taller. They travelled back together, the longest journey she had ever taken, and moved into the small house in the busy town and it was not so different, really, from keeping house for her father. When Clara was born she thought she knew what Aunt Fan had meant. Holding Clara in her arms, the bright eyes and tiny mouth, head bobbing on her fragile neck like a small bird in search of food. She lived a long swoon then, overwhelmed. It was similar with the others, when they were babies, but never the same. Looking at Clara she saw the best of herself, and her husband, and all who had gone before.

* * *

When Clara was three, William bought a second house, a rambling old place by the lake. In the summers Norah stayed there with the children and Edie, and he came on Saturdays, after the store had closed. The days were long and lazy and even though there must have been more work to do with only Edie to help, it never seemed that way. They ate all their meals together in the kitchen, because it was easier, and sometimes they laughed until their sides ached. Often in the mornings she would leave Edie to watch the boys and walk along the beach with Clara, who was now almost seven. There were other houses along the lake and there must have been other people but it seemed that she never saw anyone, heard anyone. Just the shrieks of James and Arthur fading into the sighing of the water as she and Clara walked as far as the big dead tree, pausing, bending down whenever a glittering stone caught their eye.

Summer, then, at the house by the lake, the beach house where curtains blow at the open windows in a faded photograph. The trellised veranda where the sisters are captured, grown, taking tea in long dresses, leaning back in cane chairs. If Clara had lived, she would have been one of those sisters. Married, for they all married, had children. Widowed by a war or disease she would have learned to drive, gone to church, worn gloves when she left the house. Lived long enough to complain that the world had changed, and not for the better.

But the sisters who sip tea on the shady veranda never knew her, had not even a wisp of a memory. Their oldest brothers may have, although they were young and blinkered by their own world — the sand, the lake like a vast sea. But she may have visited them in dreams all their lives; it may have been Clara who made the covers twitch.

She left the boat at Prescott, lay awake all night at Daniels' Hotel and boarded the train in the morning. The carriage rocked and she almost slept and dreamed or remembered the night before Clara took sick. Sitting in the old rocker on the veranda as she did every night when the children were asleep, the mending done. It was Friday, late, and she could hear Edie moving about the kitchen, preparing food for the next day. She looked forward to William's arrival, of course she did, but there was always a moment when she realized that the man she missed was not quite the one who came stepping down the dusty road. She smiled though at the way the children ran to him as he mounted the steps, searched his pockets for the cubes of sugar he brought them from the store. And she smiled after breakfast when he lined them up, pretending to be a general inspecting his troops. The way Arthur, who was three, tried to make himself taller, the way they all kept their eyes straight ahead while their father pretended to adjust a medal, squint down a gun barrel. It was just that his voice was too deep, somehow, rumbling through the house; his hand on her shoulder too heavy when it was time to climb the stairs.

The train rocked and she dreamed or remembered the veranda at night, the sleepy sound of insects. She heard Edie creak up the back stairs to bed, she watched the moon rise and sometime later heard a tiny noise, looked to see Clara standing barefoot in the open doorway.

'I couldn't find you,' she said, only half awake, 'but I knew you must be somewhere, so I just kept looking.'

She took Clara on her lap like a much smaller child and they rocked and talked about the moon, and she smelled the faded sun in her hair.

Her father met her at the station; he moved toward her, but only to pick up her bags. With the reins between his hands he told her how sorry he was, and asked about the journey. When they pulled up in front of the house Aunt Fan appeared and bustled her off to bed, brought her a cup of tea and closed the door softly as she left. The milk formed a skin in the cup as she lay in her old bed, knowing that it was a mistake to be there, but wondering where else she could have gone.

It all happened so quickly. The pain that got worse, and the fever. On Sunday she asked William to go for the doctor but he said what he had so often said, in company, at the dinner table. That he wouldn't have one in the house. That he and Norah were quite capable of looking after their own. He sat with Clara himself all afternoon, squeezing out cloths to lay on her burning forehead, spooning broth that she couldn't keep down.

In the evening her eyes were still blazing and they bathed her again in cool water and dried her very gently and she did seem a little better, just whimpering, now, and tired. Norah sat up through the night in a hard chair, talking and sometimes singing softly, rising only to place another cloth on Clara's head, sponge her face and neck, the water dripping loudly back into the blue china bowl. At some time she must have slept for she woke suddenly with the sound of seabirds and her first thought was that the worst was over and Clara sleeping peacefully. But then she knew, and nothing she had ever heard or seen or thought had prepared her for that moment.

People began to call the day after she arrived. The pastor first, the women of the village who had known her all her life. Most of them had lost children, most had lost more than one, and they patted her hand and told her that it would hurt less, with time. She didn't believe them; she thought she could still see the shadows in their eyes, in the corners of their mouths.

The pastor talked about Clara being in a better place; *the little angel*, he kept calling her.

But she wasn't, Norah wanted to say. Didn't say. She wasn't a little angel, not that. She had a wild temper sometimes, when she thought things weren't fair, and she wasn't afraid of anything except the dark in the middle of the night, and that not always. She would have been a fighter, Norah wanted to say, although she wasn't sure what she meant by that.

'I should have gone myself,' Norah said.

Aunt Fan had grown deaf; she had to say it, louder, again and again.

'For the doctor. When William wouldn't. I should have gone myself.'

The words seemed to hang, jagged, just before her eyes. It was an early cold but the stove kept the big kitchen warm. Through the window the trees were just beginning to flame, and when Aunt Fan rubbed her hands together flour danced in the air.

'Oh, doctors,' she said. 'It might not have made any difference at all. Your William is a clever man. Chances are the doctor wouldn't have helped at all.'

She went back to her kneading and Norah worked the fringe of her shawl. She didn't remember much about it, but she did remember William's face. When he appeared in the doorway, pushing at his collar stud, his mind already on the busy week ahead. When he saw them lying there in Clara's narrow bed. He was a clever man, her William, but she saw in his face that he had been wrong. He knew what was best, William did, but he hadn't known that Clara would die, and with her arms around her child she saw his face splinter, fall apart, and that was when she howled.

The photograph of William is familiar; he looks like all those fathers and sons who appear in cardboard boxes at auctions, at flea markets. Tight collar, carefully combed hair, a thin mouth. It is difficult to imagine him hiding lumps of sugar in his pockets for the children to find, difficult to imagine him laughing. Is that just the fault of photography? A serious business, after all. Trips to the studio, holding a pose. There are no blurred shots of William throwing a ball to his sons or walking barefoot in the cold lake, but it is quite likely that he did those things. Just as it is likely that he also felt pain, and grief, and confusion.

And it may not be fair to blame William for his inheritance; his father's stern whiskers above the surplice, his mother's black bonnet. Not fair to blame William for the state of medicine. A ruptured appendix still not a simple thing and as Aunt Fan said, the doctor might not have made any difference. It is not even fair to blame William for not keeping Norah's letters; there may not have been any to keep. His own are filled with complaints of her silence. Bewilderment, impatience and finally anger at her prolonged absence.

The letters began to arrive two days after she did. *My own dear wife*, they all began.

Norah read them in her old room, in the pale light that washed through the window. She read each one once, when it arrived, and then put it in a wooden box that had belonged to her mother. And after she had snapped the lid shut she lay back on her high bed watching the shadows of leaves on the ceiling and wondering what it was that she felt.

*You must take care of yourself*, William wrote. *Eat well and rest and come home soon. And above all avoid the draughts in that old house.*

*The boys are well behaved and Mother is managing fine*, William wrote, *although she finds Edie rather lax. I have yet to receive a letter from you, and hope that the morning's post will bring me some word. You must not brood, Norah, although I confess that I do not know what else you will be able to do there.*

*The boys miss you terribly*, William wrote, *and ask when you are coming home.*

She stopped to wonder about that. She loved her sons, but from the moment they left her arms they began to move away from her, marching down the dusty beach road behind their father.

*Still no word from you*, William wrote, *and I can only*

*wonder at your cold-heartedness. I know that you grieve, as I do, but you have other children, and a husband, and it is not right that you should abandon us in this way.*

*It is now six weeks,* William wrote, *and you have been away long enough. If you take the morning train on Wednesday next you can be on the first boat, and I will be there to meet you Friday at three. I am enclosing enough money for the fare from the dock, should you get this letter sooner and wish to leave on Monday. I cannot imagine what you are doing all this time.*

The minister pressed her hand; his was very cool, and she remembered Clara's cheek.

'You must not fall into despair,' he said, and the word tolled through her head for days.

Her father spoke of the benefits of fresh air and exercise, and she listened. She tried to go out walking but felt herself too sharply drawn, a harsh black figure in the landscape, her voice too rough and her hands thick and unwieldy. Within the house she knew this was not true; her rings slipped loose on her fingers and Aunt Fan was always coaxing her to eat. Within the house she seemed to have no shape at all, she was like a shadow falling on an armchair, crossing a threshold. And, like a shadow, making no real mark. Her father read in the evenings, Aunt Fan sewed beneath the lamp, and sometimes Norah helped her. And sometimes her heart caught, watching her hands in the soft folds of an old shirt, the needle clenched tight between thumb and finger, and she felt she was on the edge of knowing something, taking hold of something. She saw William in the doorway, as she had seen him. His fingers frozen on the collar stud, his face suddenly splintered, naked. And in the split second before she howled she had almost heard a tiny *click*, as if a door had opened somewhere. Opened just a crack, just enough to know that it was there. Clutching a needle in her father's house she thought about the door and knew, suddenly, that she would not go through it.

Clara would have, she thought. Clara was never afraid of an open door. But as the clock began to tick again, she wasn't sure if even that was true.

She went back, of course. Travelling by train and boat, the same journey in reverse. It would have been colder, but she may have stood on the deck, gripped the rail, watching William grow larger and larger at the end of the pier.

She went back to the small house in town and to the big house by the lake and she had nine more children, boys and girls. And she died not long after someone photographed her against the wall of the beach house, looking like my grandmother, who was her last. She died three years before Arthur was scattered in France, four years before William slumped over the counter in the store, six years before Bea coughed for the last time. Years before James was arrested, before Samuel beat his wife, before Janet began to drink. But perhaps not long before the picture of her daughters, taking tea on the veranda. The four sisters who all married doctors, and became the source of many gentle jokes.

And perhaps it is not her hand at all, this hand that Emma wraps around my baby finger. Perhaps it never was. But there is another photograph, one which I do not have. In it, of course, it is also impossible to see Norah's hands. She faces her child, and Clara looks up. The background is a hazy wash of sun and the fingers of her left hand are buried in the tangles of Clara's long curls, which must be warm to the touch. They are looking at each other. They are smiling.

# The Manual of Remote Sensing

The first thing she fell in love with was his name. 'Gabriel,' he said, holding out a hand at a party. And she has wondered since how different it might have been, if he had held out a hand and said, 'Chuck', or 'Steve'. Perhaps not so different; the second thing she noticed was his hand. Long squared fingers, supple, and a jagged scar snaking across the first two knuckles.

She is walking down a winter street when the words begin. Past shop windows draped with tinsel, skiffs of artificial snow. Heavy bags pull at her arms and a tin of something bumps against her left leg and she remembers Woody Allen in some movie. Slumped on a couch with light sparking from those glasses, speaking to a tape recorder: Idea for a short story. Click.

He had different stories for that scar, depending on his mood, his audience. A fight in an alley or a wound from a jealous woman, some small, touching act of heroism. He had different stories for everything but she didn't know that the night she fell in love. The night he told her, among other things, about the scar, the geese, the farm.

'My mother was having an operation,' he said.

She'd been preparing him for days, but he hadn't paid attention. When the man in the green truck came he clung to her legs, crying Why why why.

'They had to pry me loose,' he said.

They pried him loose and his mother cried and the man carried him outside and placed him on the front seat of the green truck, locked the door. Fluffs of grey wool clenched in his fingers. And the man smelled and the truck smelled and the farmhouse was big and cold. Except for the kitchen, where the wood stove burned. Where the woman with red hands lifted lids and stirred things and spoke to him in a ragged voice, through clouds of steam.

In the mornings they ate oatmeal, silently, while the early light crept into the room. Swelling the space, revealing the battered armchairs and piles of newspaper, the flat pallets of eggs, flecked with dirt and wisps of feathers. Touching the rusty tools and the bits of string lying, forgotten, in corners. He had a special spoon, rounder than the rest, and a bowl with a brown glazed design of a village. Trees and houses, a wandering stream. He stared at the bottom of the bowl until the woman told him it was time to go outside. Helped him pull on the heavy red sweater that was slowly taking on the smell of the truck, the man, the house. She spoke to him kindly and sometimes rested a rough hand on the top of his head, but he never told her about the geese, never thought to tell her.

'You know how it is,' he said. 'When you're a child.'

And she could see it all, when he told the story. Told how he lingered near the back door, scratching the hard ground with a pointed stick, saying Please please please, don't let them see me. She sees it all — the bare black trees, the stubbled fields, a curdled November sky. The red sweater, thick wool matted from washing, and his hair much lighter, hanging forward over his deep blue eyes as he feigns great interest in the tangled patterns he scratches in the hard earth by the back steps. His body tensed, clenched tight against the first faint cry, the sound that means he's been spotted. Day after day they find him, chase him if he tries to run, circle him in until he can only climb slowly, backwards, perch on the top step while they hiss around him, teasing with their beaks. Until one day he hits out with the pointed stick, brings it down wildly on a musty brown back and in an instant its mate leaps — mate or mother, depending on his audience — snaps at the stick hand, rakes his tiny knuckles, raising a long thick curl of blood.

And she sees him running and crying, running and crying down the rutted lane, past the falling-down barn. Bright flashes of red beneath a huge November sky.

She wonders about the geese, stamping her feet at a red light while a number of grey cars slide silently by. She can't trace the geese, but the farm is familiar; she went a little mad there, one long, windy spring. Walking the fields with a large black dog, the sound of crows. She remembers lying awake in a cold upstairs room, saying, Hold on, hold on. Chanting through the long, long night.

That particular version was a seduction story, and he told it very well. The motherless child, the strangeness and the fear. The way he tried to laugh about it, but didn't quite succeed. The way he lowered his head over a coffee cup at her kitchen table, looking up through thick lashes. Now she sees it all as a story, punishes herself by remembering the way her fingers trembled, reaching out to touch his hand. Now she imagines what she could not possibly have seen; a slight smile on his lips as she bends over his tender wound.

The apartment is dark and quiet, but she knows immediately that Martin has been there. A trace of a scent, a sense of things not quite as they were. He's left a mug and spoon in the sink, a folded newspaper on the table. The Classified section, with an ad circled in red: GUILLOTINE OPERATORS. *Steady employment, some shift work. Experience preferred.*

I thought you would laugh, he will say if she mentions it. No hard feelings.

'Gabriel,' he said, holding out his hand at a party, and they drank warm beer from bottles while the music thumped around them. Later they went out for a breath of air and kept on walking, all through the night. Their shoulders bumping, walking beneath ghostly trees, their fingers clasped, finally, as they walked past the shadowed verandas of the old brick houses in the centre of town. Their sandals rasped on tiny stones and they spoke to each other straight from the heart, or so it seemed.

A mean wind blows in about midnight, throwing snow and making the windows rattle. They are old and heavy, set in wooden frames; no sound gets through from the outside. Only the rattle in the wind, a ticking clock in the dark.

The first night without Martin she stretched and stretched, touching every corner of the bed. The second night she dreamed, terribly. Woke distant and heavy-eyed, turning up the radio to cover the hollow sound of her footsteps on the wooden floor. The smooth voice of the announcer, telling the death of thousands, in earthquakes and volcanoes, in clouds of poison gas. Hijackers throwing severed limbs onto an airport runway, followed by the sound of a man with an artificial heart, eating breakfast.

And she almost called him then, said, I was wrong, never mind, I made a mistake. Said, I don't mind if you fall in love, once in a while, so long as you stay with me. She almost called, but instead she made coffee, rearranged the books on the shelves. Bought a braided rug for the hollow floor. The dreams have stopped, but there is still a mean wind rattling the windows. The sound of a clock in the dark.

At work she spends over an hour with a young couple who are going to Greece for their honeymoon. They wear identical earrings, small gold crosses, and want to know all the options. Her fingers tap the keyboard, checking prices via London, via Amsterdam and Frankfurt. She watches through the long window as they cross the snowy parking lot, holding hands, until a green jeep pulls up and obscures her view.

* * *

Sometimes he called her six times a day, sent flowers to the store where she worked and once a telegram that said *Quit your job. Stop. I miss you all day. Stop.* He bought presents, wrapping her in long fringed shawls, the works of certain poets, and she stifled the small, mean voice that said it was usually with her money.

'How are you,' he said, 'you look tired, relax, put your feet up.' Massaging her temples with long, cool fingers. Making dinner, opening her cupboard doors, throwing together this and that, the way a Swedish cook had showed him, on a fishing trawler, or a café owner on some back street in Naples. She thought she would never get to the end of him.

'But I thought your father was dead,' she said, and he gave her a look full of patience, said, 'Sometimes you are so literal. What I meant was ...'

It was a long hot summer and she was in danger of losing her job, through being so often late or inattentive, and she didn't care at all.

But sometimes she didn't see him for days, a week; the telephone ringing in an empty room, curtains open to the dark when she walked past his house, late at night. Once she knocked anyway and he appeared, tousled, talked to her soothingly in the hallway but said no, she couldn't come inside.

'I told you,' he said later, 'right from the start.' And he had, that first night, walking through the scented streets.

'I seem to have bad luck,' he had said, 'with women.

'I'm selfish,' he had said, 'and totally undependable.

'I'm bad news,' he had said, tracing the line of her cheek with the tip of a finger.

In the dentist's office she keeps her eyes closed, listening to a conversation from the next room.

'But what does she want?' the dentist says. 'I'm afraid I don't understand — what's the matter with it?'

A woman's voice goes on and on in a language she doesn't

quite recognize, and then another woman speaks in heavy English.

'She says that the tooth you have made is too small. Also that it is not white, it is not a white tooth.'

'But it matches her other teeth — see? Show her, doesn't she see how it matches?'

'Yes yes, I know, but she doesn't want it. She wants a bigger tooth, yes? And very white.'

Being in the office reminds her of Martin; the reason they decided to get married, or so they told their friends. He had a job with a dental plan, she kept losing fillings. She remembers that they made a fire in the evening and lay at each end of the couch with their feet braced together in the middle. Some law of physics, perhaps, the way their feet braced together just so, not pushing one way or the other.

'Listen to this,' Martin said, turning the pages of a book he was reading. 'Just listen to this. There was a woman having nightmares, reliving a traumatic experience. And they found a lesion on the memory point, they found a scar, and they zapped it with lasers or something, and the memory disappeared. Just think of it.'

She concentrates instead on the names of the instruments. Matrix, explorer, burnisher. Quiet requests and the soft *tic* of metal on metal. The assistant sits on a stool on the other side of the chair and her uniform whispers as she reaches for the explorer, the burnisher. The drill whines, but there is no pain. Once she opened her eyes during the ceremony and saw their two faces, very close to her own. Intent, peering deeply into her mouth as if the rest of her did not exist at all.

'Is this what you want,' Gabriel said, his hands on her shoulders, his face over hers. 'What do you want, is this what you want is this what you want.'

\* \* \*

The freezing comes out slowly, replaced by a gentle ache. She sits at her desk, tapping a hollow rhythm with a pencil, writing things down and scratching them out again. Wanders the apartment, restless, turning pages, touching the telephone. And finds herself, suddenly, standing on a chair in the closet. Shifting cartons and bags and file folders, a lost running shoe. Pulling down a white shoebox, dusty, with dented corners, feeling a new pain coming on as she takes out different objects, maps and coins and matchboxes and crumbling cubes of sugar in faded paper wrappers. Pulling things out until she finds the core of the pain, a photograph, slightly out of focus. She and Hart looking at each other in front of a tiny house in Germany.

He set the timer on the camera and balanced it on a snowbank and just as she was looking at him and saying, It will never work, and just as he was looking at her and saying, Trust me, just trust me — just then they heard the click and while she looked into the lens, astonished and too late, he slapped the back of her neck with a handful of wet snow, saying, I told you, what did I tell you. And she pushed him as hard as she could and he fell, or pretended to fall, and they chased each other a little and touched cold lips and noses. They were very young, although they didn't know it.

It started in Munich; in the lobby of the youth hostel a group of laughing Americans swept her up, saying, You look hungry, you look tired, come and have dinner with us, we know this great place. And Hart was the quiet one, smiling shy and saying, Why don't you come. If you want.

She'd just stepped off the Magic Bus and nothing seemed quite real. Rattling up through Greece and the flat centre of Yugoslavia in a haze of smoke with Pink Floyd playing loud, day and night. Pausing only at gas stations where all the men were short and square and wore loose black suits, white shirts, narrow dark ties. She tried to explain the strangeness of this over dinner but the food and the beer and the warmth of the room made her voice sound far away and she stopped talking, let it all float by her.

The Americans were working in a town farther south, running ski lifts and washing dishes, changing sheets. They'd been saying goodbye to a friend at the airport, a boy named David who had already passed into legend. Good old David, they said, do you remember the time … And someone said, Where are you headed? and someone else said, Why don't you come and spend Christmas with us? and they all said, Well, even if you don't ski, it will be a great party and the town is perfect, just like a postcard, you really should see it. Maybe, she said. Maybe, meaning no. And the one called Hart sat smiling across the table, with his foot resting softly against hers.

After dinner they were all going dancing and in the cold street Hart wrapped his red scarf around her neck and said, Sleep well. And walking backwards away from her he called, There's a train every day at four. If you change your mind. And she saw the shape of the words coming in clouds from his lips.

In the morning the Americans were gone and she walked through the city, checking routes and the prices of tickets. Friends were waiting in London and she had plans; a place to stay, the promise of work. But her mind kept slipping back to a warm dream, possibility. The shape of words rising in the night. On the train she told herself that it was just talk, after all, and she planned how she would walk through the empty station and find a cheap room somewhere close, look at the mountains in the morning and be gone by noon and no one would ever know. But then the train slowed down and she saw him standing on the platform, shoulders hunched a little and dark head bare to the cold; she saw him standing like that and wondered how she could ever have doubted.

Hart came from some small place in Virginia. Where? she said, where? because she loved the sound of him saying it, and she loved it when he said her own name, drawing out the vowels and wrapping them around and around her. They stayed in a rundown cabin that belonged to someone he'd met; two rooms with stone floors and faded carpets and a long low window so they could lie in bed with a pile of blankets and the tiny electric heater glowing red, watching the snow fall. The colour of Greece faded slowly while they learned each other, where they had been and how close they had come to meeting in a dozen cities all over Europe. And they told the scars on their bodies and all their small hurts and fears and with her eyes closed she could find, easily, that place on his back that made his whole body twitch.

And the town really was like a postcard, ringed with high mountains and filled with bright houses painted with flowers and coloured patterns, the main street piled high with snow that had always just fallen. That was one part of the town, the painted houses and the clean snow and the small cafés serving tea in tall glasses. But there was also a McDonald's restaurant with discreet golden arches; there were groups of American soldiers on holiday, bright ski jackets and pink crescents of skin glowing above their ears. Four hotels named for famous generals and a PX that sold six different brands of peanut butter. How *American*, she said when Hart walked her up and down the aisles, past pyramids of ketchup, past Twinkies and boxes of cornflakes, Wheaties. But as she said it she saw that she'd gone too far. What does that mean? Hart said, as if he didn't understand at all, and he walked fast out the door and she had to hurry after him, grab at his arm, say, I only meant —

And that was when she knew that she was living inside out, nerve centres all on the surface and a word, a tone, even a certain look could make her feel such pain.

They walked and walked, still angry, past cafés and ski shops, past the butcher shop where Christmas geese hung by their cracked feet. They walked and walked and in the end, because it was late, they went into a tiny place to eat and when the bill came they didn't have enough money and they hissed and blamed each other and finally Hart told her to wait, drink coffee, while he made the long walk back to the cabin. And watching him leave she knew with a sick certainty that he wouldn't come back, that he would leave her there, bluffing, lingering over a cold cup of coffee while the owner wiped all the tables, flipped over the chairs and the sign on the door and sat down behind the till, chewing on a match and glaring while she pretended to be lost in thought. But just when she had decided that she would have to confess, to offer her silver earrings, her five-dollar watch — just then Hart walked through the door and they left with the lights flicking out behind them, door slammed and bolted. On the way home she made him laugh, describing her ordeal, and by the time they opened their own door things were all right again. Later they tried to remember what the argument was about, and said that they couldn't.

Christmas came and there was a party at the General Addams with kegs of beer and loud music, dancing, and she whirled around the floor with her hair spinning out all around, over-flowing with love for the world. She was kissing a soldier in a doorway when Hart walked by, looked and kept on walking, hard, and she had to chase him again, pulling on her coat as she went and feeling the sudden cold outside, and the silence. They were the only things moving in the mountain-ringed streets and he didn't stop but he did slow down, just a little. Come on, Hart, she said, come *on*, it's Christmas, that's all. Not even try-ing to explain about the soldier, all the soldiers, and how they looked in their clean jeans and their red Christmas sweaters, pink scalp showing through their close-shaved hair. The snow squeaked and their breath rose in angry clouds and finally Hart said he was sorry, said he couldn't believe what it felt like, when he saw her there, that he could have killed someone. And that was the night that they put a name to things and called it all love, began to say it to each other. All the next week Hart stayed home from work and they went for long walks and took pictures with his camera, sitting on snowbanks or in the old wooden armchair; they paid a fortune to have the film developed right away and pinned the photographs all around the room. On New Year's they stayed in bed and drank a bottle of wine or maybe two and every so often one of them shuffled to the kitchen, wrapped in blankets, came back with a plate of cheese, crackers, and they ate them under the covers. At midnight she was standing in the tiny kitchen, drinking a glass of water with the stone floor freezing her feet, and the moon was reflected in the sink full of cold soaking water, the curved side of a saucepan, and she heard the church clock strike, heard sudden whoops and the blast of shotguns. When she got back into bed Hart warmed her feet with his cupped hands, and she thought that she was perfectly happy.

New Year's Day they woke late, moving carefully; Hart went out walking and she washed the dishes and shook the cracker crumbs out of the sheets, swept the floor. It was snowing again and the light was grey and a little eerie, coming through the long window. Objects softened, yet distinct, and she was very aware of her body, sitting in the chair by the window, the scrubbed wooden surface of the table, a crumpled pack of Winstons, red and white, and the rasp of the match as she struck it. Through the window there was an enormous grey sky, snow piled everywhere and falling down in large soft flakes and she sat in the chair until Hart appeared, filling up the space, snow settling on his shoulders, hair, while they looked at each other through the window. He'd found a shop open somewhere, bought bread and meat and cheese, thick slabs of chocolate, and they ate it all slowly, savouring each taste, and it was only later, when they'd closed the curtains and turned on the light, it was only then that Hart said, There's something I have to tell you. And part of her had always known it, but it was the same part that had told her that he wouldn't come back to the restaurant, that he wouldn't meet the train. And he had done both those things.

Hart began to speak, in his soft Virginia voice, and he told that he'd been thinking a lot about home, lately, about a girl he knew there. You mean Denise? she said, and he said, Yes. Denise. Drawing out the vowels, lingering over the soft *s*. And he told her that he'd been thinking about himself and how he was living, day to day, no plan; he told her that he'd gone out walking and he'd gone to the *Bahnhof* and he'd called Denise and they'd both cried, or almost cried, and she'd said would he please come home. And he'd said maybe, said he was thinking about it. But you told me about Denise, she said, you *told* me, and he said that he couldn't bear it, that he hated himself for hurting her this way. Then this is all a lie, she said, and he said, No, don't think that, of course not. But it's not real life either, is it?

She took a train to London and all through the long journey she watched for him, expected, against all reason, that he would be waiting at each station. Even in London she waited, working in different places through a winter that was raw and wet and lonely, a spring that was much the same. For a time she typed letters in a Japanese bank; the men were small and gracious, forever offering cups of tea. Hands stretched out towards her, tiny silver spoons in saucers. When she remembers that time she sees cold rain falling, hears the delicate rattle of fine china.

And Hart went back to Virginia, and he married Denise and he went to law school and he called her once, years later, said, I'm drunk. How are you?

She and Martin were giving a party and she could barely hear him. She stretched the cord as far as she could, around the corner, but the line buzzed and crackled and she could hear his voice but she couldn't make out the words. She tried plugging her ear with one finger, shouting down the black holes of the past, saying, What, what did you say? Saying, Hart, I can't hear you, call back, call tomorrow. I will, he said, but he never did.

* * *

There's a clock ticking somewhere, beyond a pool of light. And she's sitting on the floor with a white shoebox in her lap, wiping at her eyes with an old red bandana and thinking that it was all so long ago. Although his name wasn't Hart. And she's never been to Germany.

# Acknowledgements

Thanks are due to the following publications, in which some of the stories in this collection originally appeared: *The Ontario Review*, *Harper's*, *The Malahat Review*, *Emergent Voices*, *Coming Attractions*, *Best Canadian Stories 92*, *The Antigonish Review*, *Carousel*, and *Sudden Fiction (Continued)*.

The author is also grateful for the support of the Ontario Arts Council.

ALEX PORTER

A graduate of York University and the University of Guelph, Mary Swan has been published in numerous magazines and journals, including *The Malahat Review* in Canada and *Harper's* in the United States. Her stories have also been published in several anthologies including *Emergent Voices* (Goose Lane, 1990), *Coming Attractions* (Oberon, 1992), and *Best Canadian Stories 92* (Oberon, 1992). Her story 'The Deep', first published in *The Malahat Review*, was included in the 2001 O. Henry Awards anthology, and subsequently won first prize. In 2002, the Porcupine's Quill published 'The Deep' in novella form. Mary Swan currently lives in Guelph, Ontario, with her husband and daughter.